Murder by design

The funeral undertaker denied all knowledge of the body in his van; it had clothes and boots on. Someone of consequence, obviously. The skull had been battered to a pulp: bone and brains all over the place.

How is it that a murdered clerk, who started at the bottom in an insurance company twenty-five years ago, comes to have a damned great painting by Constable on his wall?

The discovery of the cadaver brought Detective Sergeant Joseph Bragg of the City of London Police to investigate a possible break-in at the Cornhill Gallery, a repository of some suspiciously valuable furniture and fine paintings.

Soon he and his aristocratic side-kick, Detective Constable James Morton, had on their hands two investigations, one of murder and one of fraud on a very large scale.

Once again, Victorian London is splendidly evoked in Ray Harrison's tale of skulduggery and mayhem a century ago.

Books by Ray Harrison

French ordinary murder (1983)
Death of an Honourable Member (1984)
Deathwatch (1985)
Counterfeit of murder (1986)
A season for death (1987)
Harvest of death (1988)
Tincture of death (1989)
Sphere of death (1990)
Patently murder (1991)
Akin to murder (1992)
Murder in Petticoat Square (1993)
Hallmark of murder (1995)

MURDER BY DESIGN

Ray Harrison

Constable · London

First published in Great Britain 1996
by Constable & Company Ltd
3 The Lanchesters, 162 Fulham Palace Road
London W6 9ER
Copyright © 1996 by Ray Harrison
ISBN 0 09 475880 8
The right of Ray Harrison to be
identified as the author of this work
has been asserted by him in accordance
with the Copyright, Designs and Patents Act 1988
Set in Linotron Palatino 10pt by
CentraCet Ltd, Cambridge
Printed and bound in Great Britain by
Hartnolls Ltd, Bodmin, Cornwall

A CIP catalogue record for this book
is available from the British Library

To my wife

GWYNETH

1

Detective Sergeant Joseph Bragg, of the City of London police, peered in the speckled mirror of his wash-stand and grunted discontentedly. He would soon be forty-five, and it was beginning to show. Up to now he had put the thickening of his waistline down to beer, and a liking for good food. But the grey hairs over his ears, and in his ragged moustache, told a different story. Last night his landlady, Mrs Jenks, in one of her skittish moments, had said it made him look distinguished. That was after three port and lemons. But it had not made her any more amenable. She had still scuttled off upstairs and locked her door, in case he had any ideas. A pity. She would be a nice armful, if shrewish with it. He daubed lather on his face with his shaving brush. It had happened often enough for him to know better. He'd never get his leg over with her. And she had the right of it.

He scraped the lather from his left cheek. This razor needed resetting, as well. However much he stropped it, he could never get a proper edge ... No, they had both had their turn; both shorter than most people. She had a nice home, and memories that didn't include him. Her husband had been a dustman, with his own horse and cart; well-to-do in that neighbourhood. Tommy had not been best pleased when she had taken him in as a lodger. Felt it reflected on him, though the house was big enough for ten. But they had got along well enough; would go down to the boozer at the weekends, for a pint and a sing-song. Then Tommy had cut his hand, got septicaemia, and in a month he was gone.

Bragg rinsed his razor in the washing bowl, and stropped it briefly to see if he could get a better edge. No ... It felt as if it was pulling the hairs out one by one. He would have to buy a new one. It would be like parting from an old friend ... He laid the heel of the blade against his chin, and felt a sudden sting. Blast it!

The lather was reddening with blood. What a way to start a Monday morning! He gingerly finished his shave, and stuck a piece of paper over the cut to stem the bleeding. When he had finished dressing, he went down to the basement kitchen for his breakfast. Mrs Jenks turned round from the stove, where she was frying his eggs.

'Oh, Mr Bragg, you've gone and cut yourself!' she exclaimed reproachfully. 'Don't you get blood on that collar, it's one of your best!'

'I won't.'

He sat down at the table and picked up the newspaper.

'That Constable Morton should be back today, shouldn't he?' she went on. 'I can't see the point of sending people to the other side of the world, just to play a silly game!'

'Nor can I, Mrs Jenks.'

She brought over a plate of bacon and eggs. 'Well, perhaps you will be better tempered, once he's back.'

'Better tempered?' Bragg exclaimed. 'Since when have I been bad tempered?'

'Since the minute he sailed for Australia, that's when.'

'Huh!' It was probably true, he thought. Constable Judd was right enough. He would have done well with some county lot. But the City of London force was different – had to be. Although they policed only a square mile, the area contained the biggest concentration of wealth and commercial influence anywhere in the world. That meant it had the biggest political clout, as well. If you fell down on a case, the Commissioner could find himself hauled up before the Prime Minister. It had been known for Queen Victoria herself to express her annoyance, if some ceremonial had been less than perfect because of the crowds or the traffic. Somehow, in the City, you had to have one eye on the case and the other looking over your shoulder. That was why young Morton was so useful. He was a nob himself; the younger son of Sir Henry Morton, a distinguished general and a baronet. He knew about money, too, having so much of it himself. That meant he could read the minds of the bankers and stock-brokers. It was nothing short of lunacy, to let him go off playing cricket for three months – even if he was playing for England. Well, he ought to be back this morning. In some ways it was a blessing that Judd had broken his collar-bone, jumping down on that burglar. There should be no question but that Morton ought to come back with him again.

Bragg picked up his bowler hat and set off for the police headquarters in Old Jewry. April was promising to turn out well. A week of balmy weather so far, and no sign of a break. Not before time, either. The winter had been vile. Not really bitter, but constant rain and wind. He had three pairs of boots, and each had been constantly in some state of soddenness. He turned out of Old Jewry, into the courtyard of the old Georgian mansion that served as headquarters for the City police.

'Morning, Joe,' the desk sergeant greeted him. 'I see you've cut yourself!'

Bragg snorted. 'You want to watch yourself, mate!' he said. 'Inspector Cotton is always on about deductive power. If he got a sniff of such brilliance, he would have you out of that desk, and on the street solving crimes.'

'What, with my feet? Not a chance! Anyway, I'm indispensable. I keep the wheels going round.'

'I'm glad somebody does. Is young Morton in yet?'

'Not seen him; and he hasn't signed in.'

'Why the bloody hell not? According to this morning's paper, the ship docked on the sixth. That's two days ago!'

The desk sergeant shrugged. 'Perhaps he had some leave due.'

'Leave? He's been playing bloody pat-ball in Australia for three months! What does he want leave for? . . . Is there anything going on?'

'Not much, Joe. Do you want to look into this? Report of a broken window, in Change Alley.'

'That's off Cornhill, isn't it?'

'Yes. The beat constable reports it as being broken when he went down there at midnight.'

'What part of Change Alley?' Bragg asked. 'It wriggles about a bit.'

'The side of the art gallery place, that fronts on Cornhill.'

'Right. And, if Morton comes in, send him after me. I don't want him poached by Cotton, or anybody else.'

The desk sergeant grinned. 'A favour like that doesn't come cheap, Joe,' he said.

'Then, I promise not to tell your wife about the barmaid!'

Bragg strolled down Princes Street in the warm sunshine. The young leaves on the plane trees showed bright green; the crowds seemed good-humoured as they hurried to their dingy offices. But the traffic was just the same as usual. The Bank junction was jammed solid with hansom cabs, two-horse vans, brewers' drays. A young street-orderly darted into the tangle, to scoop up a pile of horse droppings and throw it into the bin where Bragg was standing. And these city folk thought of the countryside as being rough and stinking. In the rush hour, a junction like this could smell as foul as any midden!

When a gap in the traffic appeared, Bragg picked his way across to the Royal Exchange and into Cornhill. Looking across, Change Alley was not even a gap in the façade of the buildings. It had been built over at first-floor level, and looked more like a *porte-cochère* to a yard than a thoroughfare. To its right were the premises of the Cornhill Gallery. Bragg crossed over and strolled into Change Alley. The present buildings had been put up along the line of the medieval street. It divided to left and right before him. The buildings here were low and irregular. The frontage of Cornhill proclaimed the supremacy of wealth, of privilege; back here were the utilitarian functions that sustained it. There were several cafés, where the clerks could eat quickly and cheaply; a stationer's shop which catered for the modern fad of sending decorated cards to all and sundry. He paused and looked at the china-doll faces peering out of them, the too-perfect roses – even nests with eggs in them; as if you couldn't celebrate Easter without rabbits dressed as humans, and beribboned eggs. He snorted. That was something else brought in by Prince Albert and his heathen German ways. It just wasn't English! Somebody ought to have the strength of mind to stop it . . . But it wouldn't happen till the old Queen died. Whatever they said about her fondness for Scotch gillies, Albert's ghost still haunted the court – and that meant the whole country.

Bragg turned back, disgruntled, to the side of the Cornhill Gallery. Because of the way the building had been designed, there was no back yard to the gallery. Its side wall continued as the frontage of the undertaker's premises next to it. The gallery did not even have a back door. If there were a fire there, Bragg thought, the people in it could get fried alive. They should never have stuck to the old street plan; they should have swept it all away. As it was, the closed van in front of the undertaker's shop was virtually blocking the road – and had been all night, because there was no horse in it. He walked over to the window on the ground floor of the gallery. It was a casement, about four foot high and two foot wide. It was divided into smaller panes by glazing bars; one of the bottom panes had been smashed. It would be easy enough to reach in and open the catch that held it closed.

Bragg wandered back to the main street. The Cornhill Gallery was an impressive shop, without doubt. Its frontage was getting on for a hundred feet; great panes of glass divided by fancy iron pillars. At one of the windows, you felt as if you were standing with your back to some monumental fireplace, looking at a room in front of you. There was no clutter here, no junk-shop jumble of articles piled on one another. If you did not have a sack of sovereigns, you could keep away.

Bragg pushed through the heavy mahogany door. He half wondered if he ought to take off his bowler hat, then decided against it. He was here to uphold the majesty of the law, after all. Two men were talking at the top end of the shop. One must be a customer, for he was wearing a light overcoat. That meant the one in the morning coat ought to be the proprietor. He was tallish and slim, with greying brown hair. His voice was warm and rich. From what little Bragg could hear, he sounded like a born salesman: attentive, concerned, anxious only to clarify the needs of his customer and aspire to meet them. He glanced towards Bragg and raised an eyebrow. Bragg shook his head and began to browse round the gallery. It was a curious term to use, somehow. Granted there were pictures on the walls, even a big tapestry hanging; yet the polished wood floor was wholly taken up with groups of furniture. Fragile display cabinets were filled with delicate china and fine silver. Very pretty, if you set store by such things. Some of the tables looked as if they would collapse, if you put a decent jug of beer on them. But they would fetch a pretty penny, if the veneers and inlays were any guide.

He drifted over to the pictures. In the middle of the back wall was a big landscape. As a countryman himself, this was something he felt he could judge. A card tucked into the corner of the old gilded frame bore the name Constable, but there was no mention of price. That would have been too vulgar. Bragg stood back to admire it. You were standing on a little hillock, in the corner of a field, looking over some low trees at the countryside stretching into the distance. Rolling countryside, in full summer; the foliage heavy and dark. The meadow beyond showed more fawn than green; the sky was grey-blue, with tumbling clouds. In the distance were low hills, mellow in sunlight. Bragg sighed in satisfaction. This took him back to his boyhood in Dorset. He could almost hear the cawing of rooks, the anxious bleat of a sheep looking for her lamb.

'It is rather fine, is it not?' The man in the morning coat was at his elbow. It was the wide mouth and full lips, as well as the voice, Bragg decided. He only had to relax his face, and it naturally fell into a look of warm-hearted concern.

'I doubt if I could afford it . . . Sergeant Bragg of the City police.'

The man scrutinised Bragg's warrant-card. 'How can I be of service to you, sergeant?' he asked warmly.

'I would say that I could be of service to you, sir. Are you the proprietor of this establishment?'

'Indeed I am!'

'May I have your name, sir?'

The man lifted a quizzical eyebrow. 'Wicks, Gideon Wicks,' he said.

'Well now, Mr Wicks, the beat constable noticed that one of your windows is broken – on the ground floor, looking out on Change Alley. It would be easy for anybody to open the window and get through into the shop. And, by the looks of it, you have some valuable stuff here. We don't want to encourage burglars, do we?'

Wicks looked shamefaced. 'I am sorry, sergeant,' he said. 'It was broken by some boys larking about, on Saturday night. I fully intended to instruct a glazier to repair it, first thing this morning, but I was distracted by a customer.'

'Are you satisfied there is nothing missing from the shop?'

Wicks seemed irked by the word. 'I can assure you, sergeant, that no one gained entry to the gallery,' he said. 'Had I had the remotest suspicion of that, I would have reported the matter to the police. But I live in the apartment above these premises, and I saw the whole incident. There was no malice in it, just youthful high spirits.'

'Do you mind if I look around, back there?'

'Not at all, officer.'

12

Wicks led the way through a door in the corner of the gallery, into what was evidently a small kitchen. On one wall was a sink and a gas stove; a table and chair under the window, and a worn leather armchair in the corner. In the fireplace were some charred sticks and ashes. So this was where the spider lurked, waiting for flies, Bragg thought.

'You are quite satisfied that no one has entered these premises?' Bragg asked. 'If the window was broken on Saturday, by these boys, it might be a cracksman spotted it later and paid you a visit.'

Wicks gave a tolerant smile. 'I am quite certain. I know exactly what stock I have, sergeant. When I walked through the gallery, it was . . .'

There came a sudden commotion outside; shouts of 'Police! Police!'

Bragg burst out of the gallery and sprinted down the alley. Men were standing by the van in front of the funeral undertakers. Its rear door was now open. Another was running towards him, shouting and waving. Bragg grabbed his arm. 'I am a policeman,' he said gruffly. 'What is the row about?'

'There's a body in the van!' the man spluttered.

'Which van might that be, sir?'

'The closed van, there – outside the shop.'

'And what is surprising about that?' Bragg asked stolidly. 'Surely you use that van for collecting bodies?'

'But it isn't one of ours!'

'You are sure of that, are you, sir?'

'Of course I am! Anyway, it's got clothes and boots on!'

'Hmm. . . Let's take a look. Are you the proprietor of this establishment?'

'No. That's Mr Gibbs – over there, in the top hat.'

The group at the rear of the van opened as they approached. Bragg could see a pair of grey-trousered legs and black boots in the dimness of the interior.

'Has anyone touched the body?' he asked.

The men looked at one another. There was a general shaking of heads.

'Who found it?'

The man who had alerted Bragg stepped forward. 'I did. I was just seeing everything was all right, before I went to fetch the horse, and . . .'

13

Bragg peered at the body. It was lying on its back, arms by its side, head tilted to the left. 'Let's get it out, shall we?' he said. 'Have you got a stretcher, or something?'

Gibbs took control. 'Get a bier from inside,' he said, then came over to Bragg. 'I do hope this can be kept quiet,' he said anxiously. 'It is bad for trade to have something like this happen.'

'I would have thought it showed a deal of confidence in you, sir,' Bragg said drily. 'It looks as if only you would do.'

The bier was trundled out, and two men laid hold of the corpse's ankles.

'Respectfully, now,' Gibbs admonished. 'Treat it as if it were one of ours . . . Oh! God Almighty!'

The body was half on the bier, the shoulders still in the van. Bragg stepped forward. The skull on the right side of the man's forehead had been battered to a pulp.

'Somebody wanted to make sure,' Bragg murmured.

When the body was on the bier, he could see it was that of a man in his mid-forties. Blood and grey matter caked the dark brown hair. Bragg went quickly through his pockets. There was a slim silver watch and chain in his waistcoat, some keys and small change in his trouser pockets. No notecase; nothing to identify him . . . Yet the man's jacket was of fine material, and hardly worn. He looked like someone of consequence. And where was his hat? He would certainly have worn one, and that was likely to have his name in it. Bragg went over and peered into the van. Yes, there it was, tossed into the back. He clambered inside, and his hand brushed against something flat. A pocket-book! Out in the light once more, Bragg examined his finds. The pocket-book had been emptied of its banknotes, but there was a business card in one of the smaller pockets. According to this, the dead man was likely to be a Mr Clifford Needham, the general manager of the City of London Fire Insurance Company. So, how had a man of such importance ended up in an undertaker's van?

He crossed over to Gibbs. 'I want you to see that the body is taken to the mortuary in Golden Lane,' he said. 'Straight away, mind you!'

Gibbs nodded. 'Because of the autopsy – I understand.'

'If the pathologist is not there, tell his assistant to get hold of him straight away. I need the time of death as near as possible; we have lost too much time already.'

'You can rely on me,' Gibbs said firmly. 'And you will do the best you can for us?'

Bragg nodded and strode off towards Old Jewry.

'That was an interesting broken window you found for me!' Bragg greeted the desk sergeant. 'Don't ever give me anything more serious, or I might end up with a massacre on my hands!'

'What are you on about, Joe?'

'I had no sooner read a lecture to the shop's owner about getting the glass replaced, than there was a right rumpus outside. You know the funeral place next door? Well, they opened up their van and found a body inside. They were all of a sweat because it wasn't one of theirs! I reckon, if I had not been there, they would have dumped it somewhere and pretended they never knew anything about it!'

'Suspicious circumstances?'

Bragg laughed. 'Either he was bludgeoned to death, or he fell from the top of St Paul's Cathedral ... Big cheese, too, by the sound of it. The general manager of the City of London Fire Insurance Company, if the card in his notecase is anything to go on.'

'Do we have a name?'

'Clifford Needham. I will go to the company's offices, and get someone to identify him.'

The desk sergeant pursed his lips. 'I don't know about that, Joe,' he said. 'This is the second murder of someone working for that company in a month. The first was a bloke name of Purvis. Inspector Cotton is coroner's officer for that one, and Sergeant Jackman is working the case. Inspector Cotton might want them both done together.'

'Hey! The rule has always been finders keepers. Needham is mine!'

'That's as maybe.'

'But Cotton has not said he wants to know about any others from that company, has he?'

'No, of course not.'

'Then, I will go and square it with Jackman. Unless I tell you otherwise, assume it is staying with me.'

The desk sergeant hesitated. 'All right,' he said reluctantly. 'But

15

if Cotton comes after my balls, I shall say you never mentioned the name of the company to me.'

'Fair enough! Thanks.'

Bragg found Jackman in his room. 'I am told you are an expert on insurance,' he said jestingly.

Jackman looked up suspiciously. 'Not that I've noticed,' he said.

'Nor am I. So I could do with somebody to give me a child's guide to risks, and premiums and all that. I have never had anything worth insuring, and I have this case involving . . .'

'Don't come to me!' Jackman interrupted. 'The nearest I have got to insurance is a young clerk, who worked for the City of London company. But he was knocked on the head, going for the train home.'

'Robbery?' Bragg asked, feigning interest.

'Looks like it.'

'Ah. When was this?'

'Around three weeks ago. I reckon we have reached a dead end.'

'Oh well, it looks as if I shall just have to do my best. Thanks.'

Bragg went back to the desk sergeant. 'Jackman agrees Needham is mine,' he said blandly. 'By the way, that broken window in Change Alley.'

'Yes?'

'Wicks, who owns the Cornhill Gallery, says the window was broken on Saturday night, not Sunday night. He says he saw some kids do it, when they were fooling about.'

The desk sergeant frowned. 'Well, the constable was firm on it,' he said. 'According to him, it was intact at eleven on Sunday night and broken at twelve. He is something of a Salvationist, so I would trust his word.'

Bragg snorted. 'Those buggers have their own notion of truth. If they can believe in a second coming, they can believe anything they bloody want!'

'But why should he make it up?'

'To make interesting reading for you! Aims to join the detective division, maybe.'

The desk sergeant sniffed. 'Well, if he confesses the error of his ways, I'll send him to you!'

*

16

After lunch, Bragg went to the offices of the City of London Fire Insurance Company, in Cheapside. He had to wait for nearly an hour, in increasing impatience, because the chairman was out to lunch. Eventually he was shown into an opulent office, by a pretty girl typewriter. A stocky man with a military moustache rose from his desk and held out his hand.

'Sergeant Bragg?' he said warmly. 'I am glad to meet you. Sometimes I think that we ought to have a closer relationship with the guardians of our peace.' He waved in the direction of a chair. 'I take it that you have come about poor Purvis.'

Bragg sat down gravely. 'Not exactly, sir,' he said. 'Have you an employee named Clifford Needham?'

The chairman smiled. 'Yes, indeed! He is our general manager – and very good he is, too!'

'How long has he been with the company?'

'A little less than a year. He was appointed at the beginning of June, 1894.'

'I see.' Bragg glanced at the wall above the chairman's head. 'Is that a photograph of the staff in this office?' he asked.

'Indeed! All rather wooden – but they say the camera cannot lie!'

'So, would he be on it?'

The chairman frowned. 'Do you know, he might well be.' He got up and took the photograph to the window. 'Yes. He is in the front row, a little to my right.'

Bragg peered over his shoulder. 'Which one?' he asked.

The chairman pointed with a carefully manicured finger. 'That is he,' he said.

'Hmm . . . Am I right in thinking that he has not come to work today?'

'Ah . . . Well, I have not seen him personally. I will find out.' He rang an electric bell on his desk, and the young typewriter came demurely in.

'Have you seen Mr Needham today, Miss er . . .?' he asked.

'No, sir.'

'Would you see if he is in?'

'Yes, sir.' She smiled brightly and skipped out.

'Nice to have young women in offices,' Bragg remarked. 'A deal better than the old days.'

'What? ... Oh, yes ... Tell me, is Needham in any kind of trouble?'

'Why should he be, sir?'

The chairman frowned. 'Well, no reason. No reason at all! But when a detective sergeant from the City police comes calling, one is bound to be a little uneasy.'

'I see ... Perhaps it would be better to wait until the young lady comes back.'

'Hmm ... Very well.'

They sat in uncomfortable silence for almost ten minutes, the chairman muttering to himself and frowning. Then the girl returned.

'No, sir,' she said. 'He is not in. And he is not on leave of absence, so far as anyone knows.'

'I see. Thank you, Miss er ...' He waited until the door had closed behind her, then turned to Bragg. 'What is this all about?' he asked brusquely.

'This morning the body of a man was found in peculiar circumstances.'

'Needham?'

'I believe so.'

The chairman looked at Bragg warily. 'What were these peculiar circumstances?' he asked.

'He had been battered to death, then placed in a closed van that a firm of funeral undertakers uses to collect dead bodies.'

'Grotesque! And where was this?'

'In Change Alley, off Cornhill. Of course, we could be wrong. But we found a notecase near the body, with this card in it.'

Bragg passed over the square of pasteboard.

The chairman peered at it. 'I am sorry to say that it looks authentic,' he said glumly.

'In that case, sir, I would suggest that someone from the office should be sent to the mortuary in Golden Lane, to formally identify the body.'

'Yes ... Yes, of course. As soon as we finish, I will send his personal assistant to do that.'

'Thank you, sir. Tell me, who did he work for before joining you?'

'The Imperial Fire Insurance Company, in Old Broad Street. That is a somewhat larger company than this.'

18

'What was his job there?'

'He was the manager of their general insurance section.'

'What did that entail?'

'In the main, the oversight of fire, burglary, flood claims, as well as the routine of policy renewals.'

'And here?'

'The management and control of our whole operation, which covers much the same areas ... Oh, dear. We shall have to go through the wretched business of recruitment again. I was sure that Needham would see my time out.'

Bragg paused, then: 'How much was he paid?' he asked.

The chairman looked up in surprise. 'He got four hundred and fifty pounds per annum,' he said.

'Paid by cheque?'

'Paid by monthly cheque. Why do you ask?'

'We found his empty notecase. I wondered if anything might have been taken, that could lead us to the killer.'

'I see. Well, all senior staff are paid by crossed cheques in their name – that is to say, not by cheques drawn to cash. So no thief would be able to negotiate a salary cheque. Anyway, by now his March cheque would be safely in his bank.'

'Right ... I gather this would be the second murder of a member of your staff in a month.'

'Yes. One of our young clerks was attacked in the street, going home in the dusk. I think that, if anything, these electric-arc lamps have made our streets less safe. They throw such impenetrable shadows.'

'So, you do not see any connection between the two incidents?'

The chairman frowned. 'No! Unless some miscreant has launched a vendetta against the company. If that were the case, none of us would be safe!'

'Well, we have no evidence of that, at the moment,' Bragg said reassuringly. 'One last thing. Can I take away any personal papers, and so on, that he might have in his desk? It will save us bothering you again.'

'Yes, yes, of course.' The chairman rang the bell on his desk, and the young woman came in. 'Will you take this gentleman to Mr Needham's office, please? Tell his secretary that Mr Bragg has my authority to take away any articles he may require.'

The girl's smile was briefly replaced by a look of puzzlement.

'Yes, sir.' She turned to Bragg. 'Would you please come this way?' she said.

Bragg filled a cardboard box with the contents of Needham's desk, and took it back to his room in Old Jewry. According to the desk sergeant, there had still been no sign of Morton.

He set off irritably for Finsbury Circus, where Needham's secretary had said he lived. It was a well-to-do area. The Bedlam lunatic asylum had been torn down, and curving terraces of town houses erected in its place. In the year the battle of Waterloo was fought, it must have been a really smart place to live. Probably still was; it was bang in the heart of the City, after all. But, more and more, businessmen were living outside London; in suburbs where the air was clean, and children could grow up with green fields nearby.

Number twelve was at the end of a block. Not only was there a street lamp outside it, there were two gas lamps on either side of the front door. Useful when you came home drunk, Bragg thought, and could not get your key in the lock. He knocked on the door, wondering what kind of man Needham had been, how his wife would take the news.

The door was opened by a young maid, in a white apron and cap. 'Yes?' she asked with a smile.

'Is this the home of Mr Clifford Needham?' Bragg asked.

'It is.'

'Is your mistress at home?'

The maid pursed her lips doubtfully. 'She's in, all right. But I don't know if she's receiving.'

'Just a quick word.'

The girl hesitated then went in, closing the door behind her. Not a trusting neighbourhood, Bragg thought grumpily. But such people had a lot to lose. He would be the first to criticise them, if they let a burglar walk in. He turned to gaze across the central gardens; the trees shimmering golden-green in the light breeze. It would be pleasant to lie on the grass there, in summer; watch the clouds drifting across the blue. It was as good as the nobby areas of the West End, such as Grosvenor Square, and probably a damn sight quieter. He heard the sound of the door-lock, and turned.

The maid smiled at him. 'Will you come this way?' she said. She led him up a curving flight of stairs, to a sitting-room overlooking the Circus. 'Madam will be with you in a moment,' she said, and flitted away.

Bragg looked round the room. It was large and elegantly furnished. There were none of the solid, clumsy pieces of Prince Albert's time. It was more like etchings he had seen of Regency drawing-rooms, with gentlemen in powdered wigs and silk stockings. And pictures there were in plenty. Over a mahogany escritoire was a large landscape; something like the one he had seen in Wicks's shop, but even bigger. In this one there seemed to be a storm rolling up in the distance. The foreground was in full sun, but it clearly would not last.

'You are admiring the painting!' A woman in a stylish silk dress was standing in the doorway. She could only be in her early thirties. Was this Mrs Needham? If so, she was a deal younger than her husband.

'Yes, ma'am. It reminds me of my childhood . . . Sergeant Bragg, of the City police.'

Her eyes lit up with mischief. 'One does not think of policemen as having had a childhood,' she said. 'They seem to exist in perpetuity!'

'A Constable, is it?' Bragg said, nettled.

Her glance turned into one of respect. 'Yes. It is a prospect of Dedham Vale.'

'Very nice.'

'Now, officer, how can I help you?'

She was very good-looking, with wavy auburn hair and creamy skin. She was acting as if she had not a care in the world.

'Can you tell me if your husband went out last night?' Bragg asked quietly.

'Why, I have no idea. I went to my room at . . . I suppose it must have been a little after nine o'clock. I had letters to write. Clifford was here, in this room, then. He regularly used to bring home papers from the office . . . But why are you asking me? He could tell you precisely what . . .' Her voice tailed off.

'I do not wish to worry you unnecessarily, ma'am. But the body of a man was found, this morning, in Change Alley. In his notecase was one of your husband's business cards. The chairman of the company has said it looks genuine.'

The colour drained from her face. 'Clifford? When? Was he taken ill?'

'I am sorry to say that this man had been attacked; beaten about the head.'

'But this is ridiculous!' she cried. 'Why would anyone wish to do that to Clifford? Are you sure it is my husband?'

'We shall know for certain soon. His personal assistant has gone to view the body. But I would not want to raise your hopes, ma'am.'

She walked unsteadily to a chair. There was horror in her face, but no tears. They would come later, Bragg thought.

'Do you know if your husband had any enemies?' he asked quietly.

'Enemies? Why should a man like him have enemies?' she asked sharply. 'He was a gentle, inoffensive man. And, despite these surroundings, he was not rich. He had a good position in the City, but he wielded no great power.'

'I suppose it might just have been an accident,' Bragg said slowly. 'But the body was found inside a van, so someone put it there. Anyway, we shall have a better idea later today.'

Mrs Needham shook her head. 'There must be a mistake!' she exclaimed. 'Mildred did not tell me that my husband's bed had not been slept in.'

'Let's hope you are right, ma'am ... Do you feel up to answering a few questions?'

Her face was stony, but she was well in control of herself. 'I will do my best, officer,' she said.

'We understand that Mr Needham worked for the Imperial Fire Insurance Company, until June last year.'

'Yes.'

'When did he join them?'

'When he left school.'

'I see . . . Which school would that have been?'

'St Jude's, at Malmesbury.'

'Is that a boarding school?'

'Yes.'

'Where was his home at that time?'

She looked up with pain in her eyes. 'In Windsor. Our families lived within a stone's throw of each other.'

'So you were close as children?'

22

'By no means! He was considerably older than I . . . the age of my elder brother.'

'I see. How old are you now, ma'am?'

'Thirty-one.'

'And he would have been . . .?'

'Forty-six.'

'I see. And how long have you lived in the City?'

She took a deep breath. 'We lived in Windsor until nine years ago. Clifford used to travel up daily.'

'Why did you move here?'

'My husband was promoted to manage the general section of the Imperial's business. It was a very important post, and involved working irregular hours.'

'And he has been working for the City of London Fire people for about a year?'

'Yes.' She was twisting her handkerchief in her fingers. She looked as if she might break down at any moment.

Bragg stood up. 'I wonder if I might take away any personal documents of his, ma'am. They could be helpful to us.'

She looked at him dully. 'Of course. They will be in his desk. Joan will show you where.' She stood up. 'Please excuse me,' she said, and stumbled from the room.

Bragg put the contents of Needham's desk into a cardboard box, which Mary provided, and carried it back to Old Jewry. He raised a questioning eyebrow at the desk sergeant.

'Still no sign of him, Joe. But I'll tell you who is looking for you – Inspector Cotton!'

'Buggeration! That's the last thing I want. You have not seen me, right?'

'Right.'

Bragg slunk up the staircase, deposited the box in his press, then crept out again. It was ridiculous, he thought; and all because of the Commissioner's sense of duty. Sir William Sumner KCB had been a lieutenant-colonel in charge of an infantry regiment. He was a nice enough chap; one of those army officers who believed that, if you got on friendly terms with your men, they would enjoy getting killed for you. He acted the same way, now he was head of the City police. At first he had sought out the men

23

on the beat, the detective constables; asked about what they were doing, made suggestions the men took as orders. Of course there had been trouble – an amateur figure-head overriding the instructions of seasoned professionals. It was said that the superintendents and chief inspectors had gone to him as a body; threatened to resign unless he desisted. Of course, they had had to give Sir William a sop. To satisfy his urge to meddle, they had agreed that he should have effective oversight of one senior detective. So Bragg had found himself caught in the middle. Being operationally in Inspector Cotton's section, he had to make his formal reports through him. Yet the Commissioner had day-to-day oversight of his cases. It was a stupid arrangement. Yet Bragg had often been able to turn it to his advantage; to follow his own instincts, and play Sir William off against Cotton.

But, in a murder case, the situation became even more complicated. Legally the Coroner for the City of London was in charge of investigations into sudden death. And this coroner was intent on being more than a cipher. He was an eminent barrister; one of the senior Queen's Counsels, with a remunerative practice at the Chancery bar. He would play hell if he were taken for granted. Bragg arrived at the Temple, turned into Pump Court, and went up the staircase where Sir Rufus Stone had his chambers.

The clerk greeted him with a frown. 'Sir Rufus has an important consultation in a few moments,' he said. 'It is a very complicated matter of contract law. I would not want him distracted.'

Bragg smiled. 'Suits me,' he said. 'I do not know much about the case myself, yet.'

'Then go in. But no more than five minutes! Some of his client's advisers have already arrived.'

Bragg knocked, then stood quietly inside the door until Sir Rufus lifted his leonine head.

'Ah, Bragg,' he said irritably. 'This is somewhat inopportune.'

'Murder often is, Sir Rufus.'

'Murder?' He narrowed his eyes. 'Of whom?'

'Seems to be a man called Needham, sir. The general manager of the City of London Fire Insurance Company.'

'Ah!' The coroner wrinkled his brow. 'That company has the privilege of indemnifying my own frugal share of this world's goods, Bragg. We cannot have its servants being untimely retired from their duties . . . But you said "seems to be".'

'He will be formally identified shortly, but there appears to be little doubt.'

'I see.' The coroner rose and stationed himself in front of the fireplace, hands grasping the lapels of his morning coat. 'When and where was the body found?' he demanded.

Bragg smiled. 'Oh, it is one of yours, sir. It was found, this morning, in Change Alley, off Cornhill. The funny thing is, it had been put in an undertaker's van!'

'Huh! No doubt you will be telling me next, that it was already beshrouded and encoffined.'

'No, sir. He was fully clothed, and his hat and notecase had been thrown in after him.'

'Hmm . . . And the extent of his injuries?'

'Head smashed in at the side, sir. Bone and brains all over the place.'

The coroner's eyes narrowed. 'You will not induce me to suspend my critical faculties by such tactics, Bragg,' he declaimed. 'As you are no doubt aware, I studied medicine myself for some years, before sickening of the butchery and turning to the law. I am no stranger to violent death . . . From what you say, such injuries might equally be the product of a traffic accident. Some of these omnibuses are driven quite recklessly. I myself saw an incident, the other day. One of the horses lost its footing on those slippery granite sets. The whole vehicle slewed round, almost overturning a hansom cab coming the other way. I can well envisage a situation where some hapless pedestrian is struck by such a vehicle; and the driver is dastardly enough to conceal the happening, by placing the body of his victim in a convenient place, such as a closed van.'

'There would not be anything much bigger than a cab in Change Alley,' Bragg said mildly. 'And nothing could go faster than a walk, because of the bends.'

'The casualty could have been carried there.'

'Yes, sir. But whoever did so would have been taking a chance.'

Sir Rufus smiled triumphantly. 'That would depend on the time of the occurrence. And I deduce from your answers that you have not yet established that.'

'No, sir.'

'Then, I suggest that you do so. I expect you, as my officer, to enquire fully into a situation; and not inexpediently to restrict the time available to me, for exercising my most unworthily remuner-ated profession.'

'Yes, sir,' Bragg said meekly.

The coroner frowned. 'Am I correct in my recollection that there has recently been an undisputed murder, involving another employee of that company?' he asked.

'I know that one of their clerks was bludgeoned to death, on his way home in the dusk. Inspector Cotton is your officer for that case.

'Yes . . . I sometimes feel that the present system of selecting my officer for a case is too arbitrary and inefficient. What is the term used in the force?'

'Finders keepers, sir?'

'Yes. Smacks of the nursery . . . The ancient office of coroner has come to a pretty pass, Bragg, when its powers are so diminished and circumscribed. Those shiny-elbowed clerks at the Home Office think they can control me! Pay me a pittance, so that I have to use the police as my investigating officers, and they can erode my prerogative. But I will not have it, Bragg. I will not have it!'

Bragg had barely got back to his room at Old Jewry, when there was a knock at the door and Catherine Marsden came in. She was tall and willowy, a radiant smile lighting up her oval face. She glanced around the room and her smile faded.

'It's no use, young lady,' Bragg said in a fatherly tone. 'Morton's not back yet. The ship docked two days ago, but he has not shown up yet.'

Catherine tossed her head. 'Nothing was further from my thoughts than James's absence or presence, sergeant,' she said lightly. 'You know full well that I never come to see you on a mere social matter . . . My editor, Mr Tranter, tells me that there is a rumour about another sensational murder in the City. Your desk sergeant was most helpful. He suggested that you would know all about it!'

Bragg sighed heavily. 'What does a good-looking, well brought up young woman like you want with such muck-raking?' he said.

Catherine smiled. 'That is the function of a journalist. The public have every right to know what is going on in their midst.'

'Huh! The readers of the *City Press* would get more excited over

26

a penny rise in the price of coffee beans, than any number of murders!'

'Not when the victims are members of their own community.'

Bragg sighed. 'What do you want?' he asked.

'As an occasional correspondent for the *Star*, its editor will certainly expect from me a report of the bare facts, for tomorrow's edition. And Mr Tranter has agreed to a fuller report in due course, for the *City Press*.'

'This is all we know so far,' Bragg said reluctantly. 'The body of a man was found inside one of those closed vans used by undertakers, in Change Alley.'

'Where exactly?' Catherine asked, taking out her notebook.

'Outside the undertaker's, of course ... He had severe injuries to the side of the head. The body was fully clothed.'

'Do you know when he was killed?' Catherine asked briskly.

'Not yet, miss. But the body was beginning to stiffen when we got him out. So it must have been a fair bit earlier.'

Catherine gave a grimace. 'Has the victim been identified?' she asked.

'Not formally. But we believe it to be that of a Mr Clifford Needham. He was the general manager of the City of London Fire Insurance Company.'

'Did he live in the City?'

Bragg frowned. 'Now, I don't want you going round there, questioning the widow and servants,' he said irritably. 'Put yourself in her place.'

Catherine tossed her head. 'I would not dream of doing anything so brutal, or so unprofessional,' she said tartly. 'But I would like to fill out the general picture. And you have been glad of my assistance, on occasion.'

Bragg sighed. 'All right. I am sorry ... He lived at twelve, Finsbury Circus.'

'A good address.'

'It sounds as if he could have had an important future ahead of him. But somebody thought otherwise.'

'You do not see it as mindless thuggery, then?'

Bragg sighed. 'I don't know what to think at the moment, miss.'

'Does he leave a family?'

'I don't know about children, but I spoke to his wife. She is a good bit younger than him; thirty-one, she says. It will be hard for her.'

'Hard for any woman, where the husband was the only bread-winner,' Catherine said tartly. 'But no doubt she will not have to struggle with poverty, as well as widowhood.'

'Not if the paintings on the walls are anything to go by ... I'll tell you what, miss. You could do something for me, if you had a mind.'

Catherine frowned. 'You do not usually clothe your requests in such supplicatory garments,' she said. 'Which argues that you do not believe yourself to be on firm ground.'

'Not a bit of it,' Bragg protested. 'And, if it eases your mind, it has nothing to do with the body in the van.'

'Very well, go on.'

'I was only involved in the Needham case, because I happened to be on the spot. I had gone to the Cornhill Gallery. Do you know it?'

'I have glanced at the window display, certainly; but I have not been inside.'

Bragg gazed out of the window at the church tower, framed in swaying green branches. 'I could be wasting your time,' he said. 'But I was in there for a good half-hour, before this Needham business blew up. I was there about a window that had been reported broken. The proprietor – a man called Wicks – was busy when I went in, so I got a good look round. All I can say is that something about the place made me uneasy – apart from the fact that Wicks lied about when the window was smashed. Now, I was raised on a farm, in the depths of the country. So I have precious little knowledge about fine furniture, china and the like ... But there is something there that does not ring true.'

Catherine smiled. 'So you wish me to reconnoitre?'

'Well, it would be no use me going back again, would it? And you would be able to carry it off.'

'James could have done so equally well,' Catherine said with a smile. 'But, since he seems to have deserted us, I feel in honour bound to take up the challenge.'

'Then you will?'

'If I work at home this evening, instead of going to a party, I should be able to make time.'

'You are putting me under a great obligation, miss,' Bragg said earnestly.

'I know, sergeant. That is precisely my intention.'

28

2

Detective Constable James Morton strode purposefully down Lothbury, next morning, to Old Jewry. It was reassuring to see all the old landmarks, after three months of empty seascapes and transient impressions of Australia. And he seemed to have cheated winter. The sun was warm on the back of his neck, the trees were almost in full leaf. Yes, it was good to be back in the bustle of London; good to get away from the crowds of spectators, out of the enforced proximity to the other members of the England team. He turned into the police headquarters.

'Oh, you are back,' the desk sergeant said with a smile. 'Well done! The lads are proud of you.'

'I was only one of a team,' Morton said with a shrug. 'If any one person should be singled out, it is Richardson.'

'That's not the way we see it. It was your hundred and seventy-three, at Melbourne, that set us up to win the series.'

'Now, that has to be a prime example of southern prejudice,' Morton said with a grin. 'Is Sergeant Bragg in?'

'I saw him go up, a few minutes ago.'

'Excellent!'

Morton bounded up the stairs and entered Bragg's room. 'Good morning, sir,' he said jauntily.

Bragg raised his head. 'Ah, you've come,' he said gruffly. 'I had begun to think you had stayed behind, and married a kangaroo.'

'By no means!' Morton's smile faded. 'I went straight from the ship to see my parents.'

'Are they well?'

'Yes . . . But I am afraid that my brother's health has deteriorated badly.'

'I am sorry to hear that,' Bragg said sympathetically. 'Is it his wound?'

'Rather his general health. He developed bronchitis, after Christmas. And, mainly because he is bed-ridden, this has developed into pneumonia. He has been like that for two weeks now, and the prognosis is not good.'

'Hmm . . . Should you not ask for compassionate leave?'

'No, sir. He has all the medical help that money can buy. As for my parents, it rapidly became apparent that my bounding about in rude health was more than they could bear.'

'So you are still a refugee in the police, eh? Well, that being so, I might as well bring you up to date . . . We have had two employees of the City of London Fire Insurance Company knocked off in a fortnight. The first was a lowly clerk, name of Purvis. That one is being investigated by Inspector Cotton and Sergeant Jackman. The second is more interesting, and it's ours. I found the body myself, so I made sure I was the coroner's officer. This time it was a big cheese in the company – the general manager, no less. Here are some notes I have made. You can look at them, when you have a spare moment.'

Morton glanced at the closely written page, then folded it and slipped it in his pocket.

'Now, obviously Inspector Cotton would like to get his hands on both cases,' Bragg went on. 'So the less time we spend around here, the better. I reckon the post-mortem should have been done by now. Let us go and see what they have found.'

They hurried out of the building, and struck north to Golden Lane. The mortuary was a long, windowless building, the only light coming from the glazed roof. Grey slate slabs were ranged around the walls; some of them bore white-swathed forms. Noakes, the attendant, came over to them.

'Professor Burney is just finishing yours, sergeant,' he greeted them. 'Seems very pleased with it.'

Bragg snorted. 'He would look pleased, if he were set to cut up his grandmother!' he said. 'By the way, a young man from his employers was supposed to come down and identify him. Has he been?'

'Oh, yes. It is a man named Clifford Needham, apparently.'

'Thank God for that! By the way, you have had a sort of relation of his here recently.'

'Relation?'

30

'A younger man, name of Purvis. Worked at the same company as Needham.'

'I remember. Around twenty-eight, I would think. It must have been three weeks ago.'

'What were Professor Burney's conclusions in that case?'

'You will have to ask him, sergeant.'

'He didn't say anything to you about the wound, or the weapon?'

'No. All that stuff is above my head – Latin names and such. I'm just the cleaner-upper here.'

'All right. Can we go in?'

'Of course.'

They went through a door in the corner, to the examination room. This was Dr Burney's holy of holies. He was the Professor of Pathology at St Bartholomew's medical school, and an authority in his field. He had a round cherubic face and a wide, sagging mouth. He seemed to live in a state of perpetual delight. To see him poking about in the entrails of a corpse, with a gaping grin on his face, was enough to turn the stomach.

'Ah, Sergeant Bragg,' he greeted them. 'And Constable Morton too. Welcome home, young man. From the reports in *The Times*, it was a well-fought series!'

'We have come about Needham,' Bragg interrupted roughly. 'The coroner has an idea that it might have been an accident; being hit by a lorry or something.'

Burney's smile became oddly bashful. 'Ah! An interesting one ... But I think we can dispense with that theory completely. In such a case there would almost always be one major point of impact. Here there are several. Come and see.'

He took up a probe and beckoned the policemen to the stone slab in the centre of the room, on which the naked body of a man lay. 'See. There are several distinct lacerated wounds of the scalp ... here, and here,' he said. 'But the proximate cause of death was this large compound fracture of the skull, on the right side of the forehead. See, there are broken bits of bone and brain-substance all mixed up together.' Burney inserted his probe in the grey mess and fished out a fragment of bone. Morton looked away and swallowed hard.

'Are you saying it could not have been an accident?' Bragg

31

asked. 'For instance, being dragged along by a cart after it hit him?'

'In my opinion, no. There is no abrasion, such as one would expect in that event. Anyway, how many vehicles can move, on our congested streets, at a rate as to inflict such severe injuries on a pedestrian?'

'Only something light, like a hansom cab.'

Burney gave a sagging grin. 'No, sergeant. Even if we postulate the necessary speed, there would not have been multiple points of impact, as we have here.'

'You reckon he was bludgeoned to death, do you, sir?' Bragg asked.

'I have never seen such wounds, except in cases of homicide. And as to the weapon, I would favour an iron bar, about three-quarters of an inch square.'

Bragg mused for a time, then: 'You have recently examined the body of a young man; name of Purvis,' he said. 'He was employed by the same company as this one. Could he have been killed by the same weapon?'

'Purvis ... Ah, yes. Absolutely not, sergeant. He was killed by a single violent blow to the back of the head. In that case, the weapon was a cylindrical bar. I recall that I estimated its diameter at one and a quarter inches.'

'Ah, well. It was a long shot. Can you give us a time of death for this one, sir?'

Burney gave a moist smile. 'I understand from Noakes, that the body was found in a mortuary van,' he said.

'Yes, sir. The sort undertakers use to collect dead bodies in posh areas, so as not to upset the neighbours.'

'Hmm ... I do not think that it would have had a significant effect on the cooling process ... Anyway, the rigor and lividity alone would allow me to make a confident assertion. In my view, this subject was killed between ten and twelve o'clock, on Sunday night.'

When Bragg and Morton arrived back at Old Jewry, they were greeted by a glum-faced desk sergeant.

'You are for the chop, Joe,' he said irritably. 'Inspector Cotton is going mad. Accusing me of being underhand, letting you have Needham.'

'But I found him,' Bragg objected.

'Makes no difference! You have to go and see Cotton, the minute you get back – which is now!'

'All right. Go and write up the notes, lad.'

Bragg mounted the stairs and knocked on Inspector Cotton's door. Hearing a muffled shout, he went in.

'Ah, it's you, Bragg,' Cotton said truculently. 'What the hell are you playing at?'

Bragg frowned in puzzlement and said nothing.

'You have taken on the Needham case, when you knew bloody well that another employee of that selfsame company had been murdered.'

'I did not connect the two, sir. In any case, the pathologist says they were not killed using the same weapon.'

The inspector's face flushed with anger. 'Oh, you've got as far as that, have you? I'll tell you something, Bragg. You will push me too far, one day. You'll be out in the bloody street on your neck!'

'I was allocated the case on the usual basis, sir,' Bragg said stolidly. 'As I found the body, I was appointed coroner's officer.'

'Appointed! Don't give me that shit! No coroner has ever appointed his officer, in my time or yours. It's a police matter. And, if cases have a connection, they should be worked together.'

'I did not think the connection was strong enough,' Bragg said. 'After all, over a hundred people work for that company.'

'And two of them have been murdered, Bragg! Two within three weeks. That should mean something, even in your clodhopping mind. It's obvious somebody has it in for that company.'

'A sort of vendetta, you mean, sir?' Bragg asked mildly.

'I mean what I bloody say! Could be a lunatic, killing anybody that works for it. We have responsibilities to them, Bragg, whatever you may think.'

'I felt the Needham killing might have some connection with a broken window in the Cornhill Gallery, next door to the undertaker's.'

Inspector Cotton looked at Bragg incredulously. 'What the hell are you on about?' he demanded. 'Are you saying a crime has been committed in the gallery?'

'No, sir. I just have a feeling . . . I have already discussed it with the coroner.'

'Then bloody un-discuss it! I have a nice little case for you here. One where your intuition will come in handy.' Cotton smiled savagely. 'A break-in at a furniture repository.' He took a scrap of paper from a folder on his desk. 'That's the address . . . Just about your measure, Bragg.'

After a hasty lunch in a pub, Bragg and Morton went to Sir Rufus Stone's chambers. Being told that the great man had not yet returned, they elected to sit in the draughty area which served as waiting-room and passage. After half an hour, Sir Rufus came stalking in. He acknowledged no one, to right or left, and banged the door after him.

'He is not best pleased about something,' Bragg murmured.

They sat for a short while longer, then the clerk approached them. 'Sir Rufus will see you now,' he said. 'You know the way.'

Bragg knocked on the coroner's door, and they went in.

'Ah, Constable Morton. You are back,' Sir Rufus said warmly. 'And with your reputation enhanced. Well done!' He turned to Bragg with a frown. 'And what have you for me, sergeant?'

Bragg cleared his throat. 'Two things, sir. Firstly, the man in the undertaker's van was Clifford Needham. His personal assistant confirmed the identification.'

'Hah! Excellent!'

'Furthermore, sir, the pathologist says that he was not killed in a traffic accident, but by a series of blows to the head with a one-inch bar.'

'Did he, now?' The coroner pondered briefly. 'So it is murder . . . Did he make any connection with the killing of the clerk? What was the man's name?'

'Purvis, sir.'

'Ah yes, Purvis . . . Well, did he?'

'No, sir. He said that the clerk had been killed using a cylindrical object.'

'A bludgeon?'

'Very probably, sir.'

A look of irritation crossed Sir Rufus's face. 'Well, that intelligence hardly advances the case materially, Bragg,' he said. 'It certainly does not justify your disturbing my peace. You would be better employed in searching for the killer.'

'That's just it, sir,' Bragg said quietly. 'We have been taken off the case.'

The coroner's eyes narrowed. Bragg had expected an explosion; there was none.

'Inspector Cotton thought that Needham's case should be investigated by the same officer as the Purvis case,' he went on. 'Since both those men were employed by the same company.'

Sir Rufus Stone frowned. 'And that officer is not you, but Inspector Cotton himself?' he asked coldly.

'Yes, sir.'

'And this despite the convention which has been established, nay sanctified, by decades of usage under me and my predecessors?'

'That's right, sir. It makes a sort of sense, I suppose.'

'Nonesense, Bragg! It is a plot to thwart me, to undermine my authority, to place me in a false position. It has only the most tenuous rational justification . . . Yet it would be folly to be drawn into an unconsidered response. I will not give them that satisfaction.'

'Yes, sir.'

'There is a Latin saying, Bragg. "*Quis custodiet ipsos custodes?*" Who shall guard the guards themselves? Or to restate it, who shall police the police? I will have you know that, within the City of London, it is I!'

'Then you will reappoint me as your officer for the Needham case?' Bragg said with a grin.

Sir Rufus raised an admonitory hand. 'Not so fast! A good general fights on ground of his own choosing. They have a modicum of justification – wholly spurious, of course. But a frontal assault would be unwise. We will outflank them, Bragg. Outflank them!'

'And, how will we do that, sir?'

'Why, you will continue to investigate the Needham murder according to your own lights, and report only to me. In the unlikely event of a confrontation, I shall support you, of course.'

'And when I have been given another case to do?'

Sir Rufus looked at him incredulously. 'You will accept it, of course! I, Bragg, habitually work on six or seven cases simul-

35

taneously. And each of them in turn is given my full attention. Concentration is what matters, not continuity. Now, be off with you! I have work to do.'

'I'll tell you one thing, lad,' Bragg remarked as they left the building. 'We had better not say anything to the Commissioner about this. He'd shit himself!'

Catherine Marsden walked slowly down Cornhill, wondering how she should approach the role she was playing. She had often day-dreamed about getting married. The images had been of a white brocade wedding-dress, bouquets of flowers, bevies of brides-maids – and James, of course, looking handsome and proud. She tossed her head irritably. That was maudlin sentimentality; out of place in a generation where women strove to take their rightful place in the world ... And yet, a week ago, she had turned twenty-five. On a miserable, wet Wednesday that was totally in tune with her mood. In previous years, James had sent her flowers, taken her out to dinner, marked the occasion with a modest but exquisite present. This year he was on the high seas; there had been nothing. He could have arranged for flowers before he went, she thought petulantly. Even a present, if he really was as considerate as he pretended to be. Stupid cricket! But that was typical of men. They did not want to settle down until they were sated with the pleasures of the world. Did not need to, with many more girls to choose from. Then, raddled and jaded, they had the effrontery to choose a wife much younger than themselves. And women in her class had to put up with it. Had to accept life with an ageing roué, conscious all the time of the comparisons he would be drawing. It was all so unfair! But men would never want to change it. It would be up to the women themselves ... Why should she not take the initiative – propose marriage to James; assert her own rights in the matter? But suppose he declined; shattered all her hopes? No, she could not bear that! Better not to be asked, than to be refused ... Anyway, was she absolutely certain that she wanted him? She could certainly live a satisfactory life without him. She would never want for material things; she had a stimulating and satisfying job, was highly regarded by the men who made up the bulk of her profession. She almost had an obligation – to the downtrodden as well as the pampered members of her sex – to eschew the dependency of marriage, and live unfettered and content ... All of which ran completely counter to the role she was to play on behalf of Sergeant Bragg! She glanced at her reflection in the window of the Cornhill Gallery, and went inside.

She recognised Gideon Wicks immediately, from Bragg's description. He was having an animated discussion with an elderly couple, but she was conscious that he had noted her presence. She strolled around, looking initially at the paintings. She was surprised at the quality of them – a Stubbs, a Constable, two Reynolds portraits, a Gainsborough landscape ... Any of the Bond Street galleries would be proud to offer such fine pictures. And she had been barely aware of this gallery's existence.

Wicks came across to her. 'You are admiring the paintings,' he said in a warm, insinuating tone.

'I am astonished by them!' Catherine said. 'I did not realise that one could find such treasures outside the West End.'

Wicks gave a gratified smile. 'I studied at the Slade School of Fine Art. So I tend to specialise in paintings. Perhaps we ought to advertise our presence more ... But then, the ethos of the City is always to be discreet but discerning.'

'Actually,' Catherine said diffidently, 'I am less concerned with pictures than with items of furniture. I am to be married in the summer. We shall take a quite spacious apartment in Mayfair, and I am looking for ideas as to funishings.'

'And so much more satisfying, to select one's furniture person-ally,' Wicks said unctuously. 'Rather than leave the matter in the hands of furnishing contractors.'

'Indeed! ... I have my heart set on a salon suite in the French style.'

The warmth of Wicks's smile enveloped her. 'If I may say so, you are a young lady of rare discernment! In fact we had a five-piece Louis sixteenth suite, only a month ago. Walnut veneered, pierced crests, upholstered in fawn and red. As you can imagine, it was snapped up almost immediately.'

'What a pity!' Catherine exclaimed. 'It would have been ideal.'

'We do have a rather nice bow-fronted display case over here.' He led her to the back of the room. 'There you are! A French vitrine; kingwood with ormolu mounts. Slightly bow-fronted, as you can see.'

37

'It is most elegant,' Catherine said warmly. 'You have so many delightful pieces. I would like to come back again, when I have more time at my disposal. Indeed, I ought to bring my father also. He proposes to give me something rather special as a present. It might be a nice idea to have a piece of furniture, that I would see every day.'

'An excellent idea, madam,' Wicks said effusively. 'And, if there is some item you particularly want, which we do not have in stock, I would do my very best to obtain it for you.'

Bragg and Morton had barely got back to Old Jewry, when the Commissioner wandered in. He was short and stiff in build. Born a few years before the Prince of Wales, he affected the same close-cropped hair and pointed beard.

'Ah, Bragg,' he said, crossing to the window and staring out.

There was an uncomfortable silence, then he turned round. 'I have had the City fathers descend on me,' he said plaintively. 'Not unnaturally, they are concerned about the recent murders – two in a month. I cannot shrug it off, Bragg. Two from the same insurance company, moreover ... They are saying it will scare away business – not just English clients, but French, German, American. I have got to keep the streets safe, they say. If I do not, well, I know what to expect.'

'And what would that be?' Bragg said earnestly.

Sir William frowned. 'Why, that they would look to replace me with someone more to their liking.'

'They would never get a better man,' Bragg said, shaking his head. 'We need someone with your powers of insight and organisation, sir; someone who can make up his mind instantly – and stick to it. No, they would be making a terrible mistake if they took that course, sir.'

The Commissioner sighed. 'But these people are impulsive, Bragg. Their only loyalty is to their pocket-book. If there is the slightest threat to their profits – real or imagined – they lash out. And we are in a very exposed position with regard to these murders ... I was hoping you could tell me that we are at least making progress.'

'Ah. You have not been told, then.'

'Told, Bragg? Told what?'

'We have been taken off the Needham case, sir. Inspector Cotton was already investigating the murder of the clerk, Purvis, with Sergeant Jackman. So he has got himself appointed coroner's officer for the Needham case too. We have had to surrender the documents we took from his office to the inspector.'

'But this is unheard of!' the Commissioner exclaimed angrily.

'Yes, sir. It has always been finders keepers before. Yet I can see Inspector Cotton's point.'

'But he should at least have consulted me! I will have this out with him. Indeed I will!'

'I think it is too late already,' Bragg said. 'The coroner has been informed of the change, and he seems to have accepted it.'

'Accepted it?' Sir William echoed. 'That seems hardly character-istic . . . So we are already outflanked? In that case I, er . . .' He drifted to the door and turned. 'Thank you for telling me,' he said, and was gone.

Bragg gave a sardonic snort. 'Nothing like having incisive leadership, lad! Well, I suppose we should keep Inspector Cotton sweet, by looking into that heinous furniture repository case he gave us.' He took the scrap of paper from his pocket. 'Harp Lane. That's behind the Custom House, isn't it?'

They strolled through the balmy spring air, towards the river. Morton felt a sense of elation, of excitement. Yes, it was good to be back; good to be working with this great, grumpy bear of a man. Whatever the future might hold, for the present he was content.

The repository loomed above them like a fortress. The double doors at the front were open; a two-horse van was backed into the entrance. Bragg grabbed the elbow of a passing storeman.

'Is the boss in?' he asked.

'Over there.' The man jerked a thumb towards the back of an open storage area, on which shrouded mounds of furniture were scattered. In the corner was a glazed cubicle. Bragg knocked on the door and went in.

'Police,' he said. 'We have come about the break-in.'

The man at the desk eased the pince-nez from his nose and sniffed. 'About time, too!' he said.

'Can you give us a list of the missing items, sir?' Bragg asked quietly.

The man frowned. 'Well, there aren't any. Not that we know of.'

'But you reported a burglary!'

'No, sergeant. We reported a break-in. That's not to say there weren't things taken. How can we check, with all this stuff around?'

Bragg sighed. 'All right. Show me where they got in.'

The man took them to a small room at the rear of the building. 'There you are,' he said.

A circular hole had been cut in the window pane, big enough to admit a man's arm. The window catch was within easy reach of it.

'Have you got the piece that was cut out?' Bragg asked.

'Yes. Funny thing, it was leaned carefully against the wall, close by.'

'Well, they would not want the noise of breaking glass, would they?' Bragg said. 'The street is only ten feet away.'

'I suppose not.'

'Will you bring it for me?'

'It's in the cupboard here.' The man bent down and produced the piece of glass. Bragg took it over to the window and peered at it, twisting it in his hands. Then he returned it to the man.

'Let us know if you find that anything is missing,' he said. 'Good day.'

Once in the street, Bragg gave a chuckle. 'This will serve our turn well,' he said.

'How is that?' Morton asked.

'I don't know that I should tell you, lad. You are such an upright, honest bugger. That's why you will never make a proper policeman. You will never learn to fight fire with fire.'

Morton grinned. 'I am at least prepared to submit myself to instruction,' he said.

'All right ... It's funny what creatures of habit criminals are. Perhaps it is a kind of superstition. You do what worked last time, until you don't feel easy doing it any other way ... Did you notice anything about that piece of glass?'

'I was not close enough.'

'If you had looked along the surface, you would have seen the ring left by a rubber sucker.'

'Ah! To prevent it from falling.'

'To me, lad, that has got to be Tommy Skerret. His *modus operandi*, as Chief Inspector Forbes would say. That, and propping it carefully against the wall at the point of entry. I have run him in twice, in the last five years. You would think he would change his ways, wouldn't you? But no. It's as if he has to do everything in precisely the same way, or his luck would desert him.'

Morton laughed. 'It would appear that, on this occasion, his luck has deserted him because he has kept to his routine.'

'Maybe. He lives in the Met's area, in Stepney. Go and find us a cab, lad.'

The growler took them over the City boundary, into an area of narrow streets and grimy brick terraces. The contrast between Finsbury Circus and Stepney could hardly be more marked, Bragg thought. It was here that the servants lived, who made possible the life of luxury that people like the Needhams expected and enjoyed ... Except that Mrs Needham would not be enjoying it much, at the moment.

The cab stopped at the end of a row of dejected houses, and the policemen got down. Bragg led the way to the last house. It had an air of comparative prosperity. There were bright, crisp curtains at the windows, the brass door-knob was freshly polished. In answer to Bragg's knock, the door was opened by a plump middle-aged woman. When she saw the policemen, the smile faded from her face.

'Oh, it's you, Mr Bragg,' she said with a frown. 'Is Tommy in trouble again?'

'Well, he might be, Mrs Skerret. Then again, he might not be. But I would like a word.'

Mrs Skerret sighed. 'He's in the kitchen, washing up,' she said. 'You had better come through.'

Bragg had difficulty in restraining his laughter. Here was this hardened criminal, standing by the sink, in his braces, with a pinafore tied round his middle.

'Good afternoon, Tommy,' he called genially.

Skerret pivoted round shamefaced, and plucked at the tape securing the pinafore. 'I was only helping the wife,' he muttered.

'It's not an offence, that I know of,' Bragg said. 'We have just dropped in for a chat.'

Skerret shot a troubled glance in the direction of his wife. 'Then, we will go into the parlour,' he muttered.

41

The room was clean and comfortable. To Morton it looked as respectable as that of any law-abiding citizen. But when he took the chair nearest the door, Skerret gave him an apprehensive glance.

'Well now, Tommy,' Bragg said mildly. 'We have come about the furniture repository job – the one in Harp Lane.'

Skerret snorted. 'That wasn't no job, Mr Bragg,' he said.

'Come off it, Tommy. If that wasn't you, I'm Florence Nightingale!'

'I didn't say it wasn't me,' Skerret said sharply. 'But you can't get me for it.'

'Why is that? Did you have the Archbishop of Canterbury with you, or something?'

'I didn't go for no unlawful purpose.'

'Sunday school, was it?'

'No, sergeant. I was looking for something.'

'Something you dropped last time?'

'I never done that place before, Mr Bragg, and that's God's truth.'

Bragg snorted. 'So, what were you looking for?'

'I'd been told to look for something particular ... Not to take it, mind! Just to see if it was there.'

'And what would be the point of that, Tommy?'

'I dunno, Mr Bragg.'

Bragg stared at him coldly. 'You are going to have to do better than that, mate,' he said. 'Who put you up to this?'

Skerret blinked rapidly. 'A bloke in a pub ... Honest to God, I've never seen him in my life before.'

'And what did he say?'

'He told me to look for a French mantel clock, what was supposed to be there.'

'What was so special about that?'

Skerret was regaining his confidence. 'I dunno nothing about them, Mr Bragg. I was told it was gilded brass – a figure of a naked goddess on one side of the dial, and cherubs on the other. Oh, and it would be under a glass dome.'

'I see ... What does a cherub look like?'

'Why, they're like little angels, ain't they?'

Bragg grunted. 'And what were you supposed to do, if you found this piece?' he asked.

'Nothin'. Just tell this bloke. He said he would pop in the pub, some night.'

'He didn't ask you to nick it for him?'

'No, Mr Bragg. He just wanted to be sure it was there . . . To be honest, I thought he must be one of the family who didn't get on with the rest . . . Looking out for his inheritance, like.'

'Huh! You'll have me in tears next. Poor little Nell, turned out in the cold, cold snow without her clock!' Bragg shook his head. 'What are we going to do with you, Tommy?'

Skerret's face blanched. 'Honest to God, Mr Bragg, I'm telling you the truth,' he said pleadingly.

'Maybe. But would a judge and jury believe you?'

'I promised you, after the last time, that I would go straight – and I have! Don't I get no credit for it?' His voice was suddenly shrill. 'Blimey, next time, it will be a two-stretch! And all for nothing!'

Bragg stared at him coldly, then: 'All right,' he said. 'I'll leave it open for the moment – pretend I don't yet know who broke into the repository. But the minute you see the man who set you on it, I want to know.'

The pretty girl typewriter looked apprehensive, as she showed Inspector Cotton into the room of the chairman of the City of London Fire Insurance Company. 'I came to assure you, sir,' Cotton said, 'that the Needham case is now being dealt with at the highest level.

'That is gratifying, at least,' the chairman said. 'But are you making any progress?'

'Oh, we will now, we will . . . Tell me, sir, is there any reason in your mind, for Needham to be murdered – removed from the scene?'

'Any logical explanation, you mean? Well, none that I can think of. And, as you can imagine, I have thought of little else.'

'He had not got at odds with anybody, then?'

'Not that I am aware of, certainly.'

'Could a client have a grudge against him, because he got less than he expected, say?'

The chairman frowned. 'Hardly,' he said. 'Needham's function was purely administrative. There was no call for him to become involved in the detail of insurance policies or claims.'

'I see . . . On good terms with the staff, was he?'

'So far as I am aware, he was on excellent terms with everyone in the company.'

'Good.' Cotton scribbled briefly in his notebook. 'Can you see any connection between the murder of Needham and the murder of the clerk Purvis?'

The chairman frowned. 'I have considered the possibility, obviously,' he said. 'It seems beyond pure chance that there should be two such occurrences, in a comparatively small company, in such a short space of time. Yet I have been able to discover not the remotest linkage between the two. From what I am told, Purvis was very bright and diligent; but he was a junior clerk, concerned with the detail of household policies. On the other hand, Needham was involved in the higher management of the whole company. There was no reason why he should have even been aware of Purvis's existence.'

'And no reason why some third party should have had it in for both of them?'

'No, inspector. I can see no rational link between the two occurrences. And I would hate to think that some madman is set on a course of murdering officials of insurance companies in general, or this one in particular.'

Cotton smiled indulgently. 'I don't think you need to worry about that, sir,' he said. 'In my experience, there is always a good reason for murder.'

The chairman snorted. 'The day you have Jack the Ripper behind bars, inspector, that day I may believe you.'

Cotton cleared his throat. 'Yes, well, that case is a one-off . . .' He flipped back through his notebook. 'It would appear that both Purvis and Needham were killed in the street, and during the hours of darkness.'

'Well, dusk in the case of Purvis.'

'Where Needham was concerned, the money was removed from his notecase, but his watch was left on the body. Do you see any significance in that, sir?'

The chairman frowned. 'Presumably it would have taken too much time to remove the chain from his waistcoat.'

'Yes. Except that whoever did it had time to put the body in the undertaker's van.'

'Indeed. But not time to do more, perhaps.'

'Right, sir.' Cotton tried another tack. 'We might conclude that, because Needham's business card was left in the notecase, his assailant was making no attempt to conceal his victim's identity.'

'That is near to arguing a totally random killing,' the chairman said irritably.

'But it could be that the murderer just wanted us to think that ... How long had Mr Needham been employed by this company, sir?'

'Since June of last year.'

'Only ten months? And he came here from the Imperial?'

'Yes.'

Cotton pondered, then: 'Was there anyone else in the running for the job?' he asked.

The chairman hesitated. 'As a matter of fact,' he said, 'two of our existing senior managers were considered – even to the stage of the final interview board. But neither of them had the breadth of experience that Needham possessed.'

'I see, sir. Could you give me the names of these two gentlemen?'

'Of course. Denison and Hunter. You may speak to them, if you so wish. Frankly, I cannot conceive that they could have had any hand in this terrible affair. After all, the three of them have worked together harmoniously for the best part of a year.'

Cotton got to his feet. 'Maybe, sir,' he said. 'But human nature is a funny thing isn't it?'

3

When Bragg got to his room, next morning, he found Morton tidying the drawers of his desk.

'Spring cleaning?' he asked drily.

Morton grinned. 'Part of the process of settling in,' he said.

'What we need, lad, is for you to write a bit of fiction. Some notes about the Tommy Skerret business, that will give us time to poke about on the Needham murder.'

'That would hardly be easy, if Skerret was right about his not having committed any crime.'

'Hmm . . . We will have to check that. But he seemed sure of his ground, I'll allow.'

'Yet even if that is true, it need not inhibit us. We could still claim to have information – perhaps about a crime in the process of being committed.'

'You've lost me, lad,' Bragg said, taking his pipe from his pocket and pulling it apart.

'In Monday's *Times* there was a report of the theft of large denomination banknotes, from a Birmingham bank. We could put it about that we have information about that.'

'From a nark, you mean?'

'Yes. Information to the effect that Skerret is involved in distributing them; to people who will convert them into smaller denomination notes. After all, one could hardly think of a better place to conceal banknotes than in a blanket-box, under a dust-sheet, in a pile of furniture in a repository.'

'But, accepting that, why wouldn't we go in and tear the place apart?' Bragg asked, inserting a pipe-cleaner in the stem of his briar.

'Because our aim is to catch the whole gang. We do not wish to alarm them before the crucial moment.'

46

'Hmm ... Would Inspector Cotton buy that one? He's no fool, even if he is an uncouth pig.'

'For long enough, I hope.'

'It might work. But who did we get our information from?'

'A source we cannot reveal!'

Bragg snorted. 'The Commissioner might swallow that, but no one else would. Still, we are working to him, and there doesn't seem much option. All right, do something on those lines. We need not mention it unless we have to.'

There was a tap at the door, and Catherine Marsden came in. 'Good morning, sergeant,' she said. She was wearing the blue tailor-made and white jabot which constituted her working clothes. A small hat nestled among her upswept curls. 'And Constable Morton, returned from the antipodes crowned with laurels!'

'Good morning, Miss Marsden!' Morton said, a delighted grin on his face.

'We had resigned ourselves to your staying in Australia for ever, had we not, sergeant?' Catherine said lightly.

'Never!' Morton protested. 'After three months of male company – cricketers moreover – I long for intelligent, informed conversation. And if beauty and wit accompany it, why, I might almost become civilised again!'

'You are still as *gallant* as ever, James.' Catherine gave a dismissive toss of the head.

'Have you anything for me, miss?' Bragg interrupted gruffly.

Catherine seated herself on the chair opposite them. 'I did as you requested, sergeant,' she said lightly. 'I went to the Cornhill Gallery, giving as my pretext that I was about to be married.' She glanced sideways at Morton, but he was staring out of the window. 'I even wore one of my mother's diamond rings on my engagement finger, to support the pretence.'

'You are a marvel, miss! A real sport!' Bragg said warmly. 'So how did you get on?'

'Frankly, sergeant, I was astonished at the quality of the goods on display. Did you see that Japanese Imari dish?'

'I would not have recognised it, if I had,' Bragg said gruffly.

'And there was a beautiful five-drawer chest, in walnut oyster veneers. I certainly coveted that! Indeed, had my pretext been a reality, I could have virtually furnished my apartment. And with

47

choice pieces, moreover! I am sure that, if James were to visit the gallery, he would confirm my impressions.'

'Hmm . . .' Bragg was cutting thin slices of tobacco from a rope of twist. 'So you could not see anything odd about the place?' he asked.

Catherine smiled. 'The only oddity is that it should be there at all; rather than in the West End, with all the other fashionable shops.'

'That had struck me, too, miss.' Bragg began to rub the tobacco between his palms, and feed it into his pipe.

'Mr Wicks gave me an explanation that I suppose is valid,' Catherine said. 'He remarked, rather enigmatically, that the City is discreet but discerning.'

'You mean, he can get West End prices with little or no effort?'

'Presumably so – provided that the quality is there.'

Bragg leaned back in his chair and struck a match. He laid it across his pipe and began to puff clouds of smoke about his head. Then he grunted with satisfaction. 'You remember I said I was uneasy about the place, miss?' he said.

'Yes.'

'I was thinking about it, all last night. I decided it was the pictures. Did you get a good look at them?'

'I saw the Constable and the Gainsborough – oh, and some Reynolds portraits.'

'It wasn't them,' Bragg said pensively. 'I enjoyed them . . . Interestingly enough, there is a Constable with much the same sort of scene, in Needham's drawing-room . . . No, it was the one with the couple in a trap. There seemed to be something not quite right about it.'

'The Stubbs?' Catherine asked. 'Yes, I did see that. And I must confess that it seemed perfectly charming to me.'

'So you would go along with the names on the cards, miss.'

Catherine hesitated. 'I cannot pretend to be as expert as my father. Perhaps we ought to persuade him to go there! If it takes a thief to catch a thief, it might take a painter to evaluate a painter. As for me, I would be content to accept the attributions.'

'So they would be worth a fortune, eh?'

'Yes indeed! But then, everything in the gallery is of high value.'

'Including a Constable?'

'Especially a Constable.'

48

Bragg laid his pipe in an ashtray. 'In that case, miss, we seem to have something of a conundrum. How is it that a clerk, who started at the bottom in an insurance company, around twenty-five years ago, comes to have a damn great Constable on his wall?'

When Bragg arrived outside the coroner's court, later that morning, he mingled with the usual collection of sensation-seekers and idlers. For them, an inquest was the nearest thing to a Roman circus. He could see Inspector Cotton talking animatedly with a group of newspaper reporters. Stupid idiot, Bragg thought uncharitably. He was so keen to get his name in the papers, he never once thought they would crucify him if he did not get results. Bragg could see Henley of the *Daily Chronicle* and Figgis of the *Echo*. Neither of those papers was well disposed towards the City. Cotton was storing up trouble for all of them.

When the crowd drifted into the court, Bragg lingered until Cotton had gone in. Then he found himself a place at the end of a pew-like bench. It was an impressive chamber, there was no denying that. The City's coat of arms, in scarlet and gold, dominated proceedings. Below it was the coroner's desk, on a high dais. To the left his clerk was swearing in a jury. Bragg noted sardonically that Inspector Cotton had taken a seat within a yard of the witness-box. He would certainly hear every word; though what he would make of them was anybody's guess.

Precisely on eleven o'clock, the clerk rapped twice with his gavel. There was a great shuffling of feet, as those present stood up. A bewigged Sir Rufus Stone came billowing into court, a stern look on his face. He ascended the steps to the dais, placed his papers on his desk, bowed to the assembly and sat down.

'In the matter of Clifford Needham, deceased,' the clerk announced.

Sir Rufus glared about him as the public settled themselves. 'Who gives evidence of identity?' he asked.

An usher bustled towards a young man sitting on the front row, and escorted him to the witness-box.

'Your name?' Sir Rufus asked curtly.

'Archibald Young.'

'Are you related to the deceased?'

'No, sir.'

'Then, in what capacity were you able to identify the body?'

Young licked his lips nervously. 'I worked with him, my lord.'

Sir Rufus gave a wolfish smile. 'Our gracious Queen has not yet seen fit to ennoble me, Mr Young. "Sir" will be quite adequate.'

'Yes, sir.'

'Would you say that you knew the deceased intimately?'

'I was his personal assistant. I knew him well, yes.'

The coroner made a note, then: 'Have you been shown the body of a man, at the City mortuary?' he asked.

'Yes, sir.'

'And, are you satisfied that it is the mortal remains of your colleague, Mr Needham?'

'I am.'

'Very well, Mr Young. You may step down.'

The clerk stumbled from the witness-box, his face strained.

'I will now take evidence of discovery,' the coroner proclaimed.

Bragg got up and went into the witness-box. 'Joseph Bragg, detective sergeant, City of London police,' he announced.

The coroner looked at him coldly. 'Will you briefly state the circumstances surrounding your discovery of the body, which we now know to have been that of Mr Clifford Needham?'

'Yes, sir. I had gone to the premises of the Cornhill Gallery, on an unrelated matter. While I was there, I heard agitated shouting in Change Alley. I went to investigate, and saw a group of men around the rear of a funeral undertaker's van. Inside the van was the fully clothed body of a man.'

The coroner frowned. 'If that be the case, then it would appear that you did not discover the body at all,' he said coldly.

'If we are to be absolutely accurate, sir, that is true.'

Sir Rufus leaned back in his chair and fixed Bragg with a baleful glare. 'Are you telling me,' he declaimed, 'that the police have become reckless of fact, heedless of the truth? Of course we must be absolutely accurate! How can this, or any court, return a true verdict, if evidence is presented to it in such a slipshod fashion? Who actually made the discovery?'

'An employee of the undertaker's business, Mr Alfred Simmons, sir.'

'And why is he not here to give evidence of the fact?'

'He has had a nervous breakdown because of it, sir.'

A look of incredulity spread over the coroner's face. 'Are you telling the court that Mr Simmons, who is habituated to handling the bodies of deceased persons during the course of his employment, has been so affected by this incident, as to be unable to attend this court and give evidence on the matter?'

'That is the case, sir. I gather that it was because the body was not one of theirs.'

There was a titter at one side of the court. Sir Rufus swung round, and glared in that direction till it subsided.

'I am well appraised of the desirability that inquests into unexpected deaths should be subject to public scrutiny,' he said coldly. 'Nevertheless, if there is any repetition of this unseemly levity, I shall clear the court.'

He turned back to Bragg. 'And why do you consider yourself qualified to give valid evidence of discovery, sergeant?' he asked.

'I heard the shouting, sir, and ran across. A group of men was forming round the van. The rear door was open. In my opinion, the body had not been moved.'

'And how does your opinion assist the court?'

'I believe that, in the absence of Mr Simmons, I am as well qualified as any of the others to give evidence of discovery.'

Sir Rufus frowned. 'Very well,' he said. 'At what time was the discovery made?'

'Twenty-three minutes to ten o'clock, on the morning of Monday the eighth of April, sir.'

The coroner's eyes narrowed. 'You are able to be so precise, sergeant?' he asked.

'Yes, sir. I immediately looked at my watch, when I heard the shouting.'   -

The coroner gave him an icy stare, then: 'Very well, you may stand down.'

There was a murmur of conversation, a shuffling of feet, then the bang of the clerk's gavel. 'Call Inspector Cotton,' he said.

Reaching his seat, Bragg saw Cotton start to his feet, a mixture of incredulity and apprehension on his face. He walked reluctantly to the witness-box.

The coroner turned to his clerk. 'We will take the evidence of this witness on oath,' he said.

Sir Rufus sat impassively as Cotton went through the oath. Then he leaned forward. 'You, Inspector Cotton, are the coroner's officer in this case – my officer,' he said.

Cotton contrived a half-smile. 'Yes, sir,' he said.

'It is now three days since the murder of this worthy citizen. Have you established a motive for the killing?'

A look of incomprehension spread over the inspector's face. 'It's early days, yet, sir,' he mumbled.

'Is that remark intended to convey to the court that you have discovered nothing?'

'I wouldn't exactly say that, sir.'

'Then, what would you say?'

Cotton licked his lips nervously. 'The deceased was struck down, late at night, by someone using a blunt instrument.'

'Go on,' the coroner prompted, a malicious smile on his lips.

'Then someone must have put the body in an undertaker's van.'

'And who, in your view, is that someone?'

'Well, sir, it could be the murderer; or it could be someone else.'

'Which someone else?'

Cotton moistened his lips with his tongue. 'Why, anyone.'

The coroner frowned in exaggerated puzzlement. 'Are you suggesting that any worthy citizen, walking along Change Alley late on a Sunday night, in pursuit of his legitimate interests, and coming upon the battered body of a fellow inhabitant of this great city, might be so remiss as to pick up the corpse, place it in an undertaker's van and continue on his way?'

'People do funny things, sir,' Cotton mumbled. 'You'd be surprised.'

'Do you not regard it as more likely,' the coroner said tolerantly, 'that it was the action of the killer, to conceal his foul deed?'

Cotton seemed to be recovering his equilibrium. 'I think, if I had battered somebody like that, in an empty street, I would have run for it,' he said.

Sir Rufus looked at him coldly. 'Yes, I believe you would,' he said. 'Have you given any consideration as to the motive for this crime? Or have you already determined that it was a random killing which merits scant attention?'

Cotton frowned. 'Well, sir,' he said doggedly, 'I suppose he could have had enemies.'

'What enemies?' the coroner demanded.

'When he got his present job, two existing employees of the City of London Fire Insurance Company were in the running; a Mr Denison and a Mr Hunter.'

The coroner was momentarily aghast. 'The jury will disregard that answer,' he said hastily. 'The hearing is adjourned, *sine die*!' He got to his feet and swept out of the court.

Cotton crossed over to Bragg. 'That's the way to handle Sir Rufus,' he said smugly. 'He thought he could screw my balls off; but I showed the bugger. He won't try to put it across me again!' He marched triumphantly out of the court.

Bragg waited for five minutes, then knocked on the door of the coroner's robing room. As he went in, Sir Rufus was engaged in placing his wig on its stand.

'Well, Bragg?' he said irritably. 'What is it that you want? I have a conference, in half an hour, on a particularly complex matter.'

'You will be in good form, then, after twisting Inspector Cotton's tail like that,' Bragg said innocently.

Sir Rufus gave him a searching look. 'The police have to be put in their place from time to time,' he said curtly.

'Yes, sir . . . I wonder if I might pick your brains about a point of general law, sir?'

'If it is a matter of Chancery law, my clerk will bill you!' the coroner said, regaining his good humour.

'I will take that risk, sir . . . There has been a break-in at a furniture repository. Nothing was taken. Now, we know the man who did it. Moreover, he admits it. But he says we cannot charge him, because he was not intending to steal anything. He had been asked to get in there and look round. Somebody wanted to know if a particular clock was there.'

'It sounds like the needle in the proverbial haystack!'

'Yes, sir. According to our man, he could not find it – hardly knew where to start. So he clambered back out of the window and went home.'

'Taking nothing from the premises?'

'Right.'

'And you believe him, Bragg?'

'Yes . . . Yes, I do.'

'Very well. Then there was clearly no felonious intent, so the act amounts to mere intrusion. It would appear that we are left with trespass – hardly a hanging matter! I suppose the warehouse is not part of a railway installation, or an adjunct of a powder magazine?'

Bragg smiled. 'We can be sure of that, sir.'

53

'Why, then, you have nothing, Bragg. If you took the matter further, you would be wasting your time.'

Bragg got back to Old Jewry to find Morton sitting at his desk, regarding a drawing with considerable satisfaction.

'What the hell is that?' he asked, throwing a newspaper on his desk.

Morton smiled. 'The first stage of the Skerret diversionary operation! This is the floor plan of the repository, as far as I can remember it. The squares represent various piles of house contents; but I have to confess that they bear little relation to the actuality. However, the window is in more or less the right position.'

'You missed a bit of fun, lad,' Bragg said smugly.

'Not voluntarily, I assure you, sir!'

'No ... It would not have been right for you to be there. A bad example. I think our beloved coroner was well and truly niggled, when Cotton took us off the case. So he decided to get his own back.'

'How?'

'Well, you know these initial coroner's hearings are usually routine. Identity, discovery, then bang, let's all go home ... But this time, Sir Rufus calls his officer to give evidence.'

'Inspector Cotton?'

'Yes – and on oath into the bargain. You should have seen the look on Cotton's face! Particularly when the coroner started quizzing him on what he had discovered. Made the inspector look like a complete idiot ... Mind you, it was deserved. Cotton has done bugger all on the case, since he took it off us.'

'Then, he is running true to form.'

'All the same,' Bragg said, 'the open court was not the place to haul him over the coals. And I reckon the inspector decided to hit back. So, when the coroner asked him if Needham had any enemies, Cotton gave him the names of the two employees of the insurance company, who had been in the running for his job.'

'Exceedingly prejudicial!'

'I've never seen a hearing closed down so quickly, in my whole life! The only pity is that Cotton thinks he had the best of it. But, with any luck, the Commissioner will have writs for defamation flying round his head tomorrow!'

Morton grinned. 'Nevertheless, it is possible that Inspector Cotton penetrated down to levels of iniquity that did not yield to our feeble burrowings!'

'Not from the sound of it.'

Bragg picked up his newspaper. 'Let us see what the *City Press* obituary has to say about our man.'

'Nothing but good, if it is running true to form,' Morton said.

'Here we are ... Aged forty-six. Came from an old Windsor family, according to this. The eldest of three brothers ... joined the Imperial Fire Insurance Company in 1868 ... various posts held. Then went to the City of London company last year, as general manager. Married 1884. Leaves a widow, Alice. No issue. Private funeral at Windsor on Thursday ... That's the lot, lad.'

'With such a meagre offering, his death was obviously not expected,' Morton remarked.

'Or the general manager of that particular company is of no account ... Yet it is an important concern. Its general manager ought to count for something. And, after all, Needham has been in the City all his working life; made his way up from the bottom. He's just the sort of man that City folk like to pay tribute to.'

Bragg picked up the cardboard box holding the contents of the desk at Needham's residence, and emptied it on Morton's table. 'A good thing Inspector Cotton did not demand this lot from us, lad,' he said.

Morton smiled. 'Could that result from the fact that we neglected to inform him of its existence?' he asked.

'I don't like the word "neglected". They shoot you for that ... Now, what have we here? Ah, his will. Take a look at that, lad. It's more in your line.'

Bragg sorted out the jumble of paid bills, bank books, letters.

'The will seems very straightforward,' Morton said at length. 'Apart from trifling legacies to servants, all his assets will go to his wife.'

'Can you see her knocking him off, lad?'

'Not having had the pleasure of meeting the lady,' Morton said, 'I can hardly comment!'

'Good thing, too! She's a real beauty. Turn any young fellow's head ... What would have happened if she had died first?'

'All left equally to his brothers, or their lawful heirs. Perfectly normal. And nothing could turn on that, so long as Mrs Needham

55

was alive ... However, it does show that they had no children; even that they did not expect to have any.'

'I suppose that is true,' Bragg murmured. 'Ah, here is the lease of their house ... and a pretty penny it was costing him. That's odd. It is dated in 1886 – eight years before he was recruited by his last employers.'

'While he was still with the Imperial?'

'Yes. I find that surprising, somehow. I know he was a senior employee there; but that is all he was ... I wonder how long he has had that painting.'

'The Constable? Perhaps he inherited it,' Morton suggested.

'What, with two brothers in the running as well?'

'The Needhams could be a wealthy family.'

Bragg pondered. 'No, lad, I don't see that. Our man started as a clerk in an insurance company. That is not the way rich folk do things ... Ah!' He picked up a small bundle of bank pass-books, held by an elastic band. 'The Colonial bank in Bishopsgate. Sounds about right, for a City man.' He flipped rapidly through them ... 'Interesting.'

Morton crossed to look over his shoulder. There were quarterly withdrawals which tallied with the rental due under the Finsbury Circus lease. There were also frequent cash withdrawals, some for substantial amounts.

'This account was opened just before the Needhams moved to their present house,' Bragg said. 'Now, look at the credits. Here are the monthly salary cheques going in. But look at these! Transfers from "N.P. Windsor".'

'Presumably from the National Provincial bank's branch in Windsor,' Morton said.

'Yes. But look at the size of them!' Bragg picked up the earlier books and thumbed through them. 'Here we are!' he exclaimed. 'They start as far back as '86, practically as soon as the account was opened.'

'There may be nothing remotely sinister in it,' Morton said.

'You still harping on that family wealth?' Bragg said exultantly. 'No, lad. There's something wrong here. I feel it in my bones.'

4

When Bragg got to his room in Old Jewry, next morning, Morton was scribbling away industriously.

'What is that?' he asked.

Morton looked up with a grin. 'The great Skerret intrigue,' he said. 'I am speculating as to how one-hundred-pound notes could be most discreetly converted into smaller denominations.'

'Oh?'

'Obviously, no one would tender such a note in return for an ounce of tobacco! As I see it, we have two essential requirements. Firstly the establishment must be involved in activities where the clientele habitually pays with high-denomination notes. Secondly, the activities must be of such a nature as to attract men of ample means.'

'Sounds like two sides of the same coin,' Bragg said grumpily.'So what are we looking for?'

Morton wrinkled his brow. 'The old stand-bys, I suppose. Race-tracks, gambling clubs . . .'

'Brothels? I can see you having a rare old time, lad, if we have to maintain the pretence.'

'I would not be so churlish as to keep the field-work entirely to myself, sir!' Morton said with a grin. 'And I think I would be more fitted to take on the gambling side.'

'Huh! . . .' Bragg tugged at his ragged moustache. 'D'you know,' he said, 'for all that I've been a widower twenty-two years, I've never been in a brothel in my life. I wouldn't know how to start . . . But I have laid a bet or two!'

There came a diffident tap on the door, and the Commissioner came in.

'Ah, Bragg.' he said dolefully. 'I suppose you have not yet seen the report.'

'Report, sir? What's that?'

'In the *Chronicle*. There is what I can only describe as an attack on me personally, in this morning's edition.'

'On you, sir?' Bragg said in a shocked tone.

'Well, I was not actually named; but the conduct and competence of the City force was laid open to question. That is bound to redound to my personal discredit.'

'I don't believe it, sir!' Bragg said earnestly. 'We have never had a Commissioner who was so highly regarded by the men.'

'Perhaps that is part of the problem,' Sir William said mournfully. 'Coming as an outsider, I have to take the loyalty of the men on trust. To a great extent, I must also assume that they are competent to discharge the tasks appropriate to their rank. Both those matters are laid open to question.'

He crossed over to the window and peered out.

'What was this report about, sir?' Bragg asked quietly.

'Why, the Needham inquest.'

'Ah, yes. I saw Henley, the reporter, was there.'

The Commissioner turned round with a sigh. 'I frankly do not know what to believe, Bragg. Inspector Cotton complains that the coroner called him to give evidence, without warning. That, in the course of a hostile examination, he demanded to know if Needham might have had enemies . . .'

Bragg broke the growing silence. 'That can hardly be down to you, sir,' he said.

Sir William gave a pained smile. 'The *Chronicle* does not agree with you,' he said. 'Indirectly, I am accused of laxity and incompetence. The article stopped short of demanding my resignation, but only just.'

'Well, that's not fair, sir,' Bragg said piously. 'If anything was out of order, it was the coroner's fault. He called his officer, and he questioned him.'

The Commissioner looked sideways at Bragg. 'This was the case where Inspector Cotton took control of the investigation, and replaced you as coroner's officer, was it not?'

'Yes, sir.'

'But I gather that you were present at the hearing.'

'Just giving evidence of discovery, sir.'

'And, is it true that Inspector Cotton named two City figures as being under suspicion of murdering Needham?'

Bragg shook his head. 'That is not true,' he said emphatically. 'Sir Rufus Stone was trying to establish what progress there had been. He asked the inspector if Needham had any enemies – pressed him on it. Inspector Cotton said that two officials of the City of London Insurance Company had been in line for the general manager's job, as well as Needham.'

'Yes. But I gather that he named them.'

'Yes, sir. Denison and Hunter.'

'So the *Chronicle* said . . . I tell you, Bragg, an unholy rumpus is building up. I had the chairman of the insurance company ringing me on the telephone system, this morning. He was ranting on about the inefficiency of the force, scapegoats and false accusations . . . I tell you, they are after my head, Bragg. He even threatened to sue me for defamation!'

'Well, sir,' Bragg said quietly, 'whoever is at fault in this, it is not you personally. If I were you, I would not give them the satisfaction of having got rid of you. We are not policing some rough North-Country mill-town. The City needs someone intelligent and sensitive at the head of the force. I don't believe we have had anyone to touch you, in all our history.'

The Commissioner gave a sheepish smile. 'Well, it is good to know that I can count on the loyalty of the men,' he said, and wandered out.

'So you got your wish, sir,' Morton said with a smile.

'Wish, lad? No, not wish. Not that blame should fall on Sir William . . . Now, then, I'm off to Needham's funeral.'

'Are you assuming that we shall see his killer there?'

'No, lad. Not we. You stay home and mind the shop. If you have any time left over when you've finished your fairy story, pop down to the Cornhill Gallery. See what you think about the place.'

Catherine reached Windsor just after half-past eleven. She acknowledged that she was feeling slightly smug. Mr Tranter, her editor, had admitted that the murder of Needham had generated exceptional public interest. And the scurrilous outburst in that morning's *Chronicle* could only increase it. So he had reluctantly acceded to her suggestion that she should write a more general article on Needham, from a woman's standpoint. Whether attending his funeral would amplify the material available to her, was open to debate. But his widow and family members would be there; she would at least know what they looked like, when she wrote her piece.

As she left the railway station, the massive bulk of the castle seemed to dwarf every building around. Even the church seemed like a child's toy, in its shadow. A group of men stood at the porch, their hats draped with black crape. One of them nodded to her, as she walked gravely into the church. She was surprised to see an elaborate ebony coffin, on trestles in the chancel. But, of course, Needham's body would have been brought by train, from London, the previous night.

The church was already filling. Catherine squeezed into a place three pews behind the empty front rows, where the mourners would sit. Around her were men in black frock coats and black ties; City luminaries showing solidarity with a fallen comrade. Some of them exchanged muttered remarks. But most sat mute – perhaps apprehensive that Needham's fate might befall them.

The organ began to play softly. Catherine did not recognise the music. Perhaps she ought to ask the organist to identify it for her, after the service . . . She had not quite decided what slant to give to her article. Should it be coldly factual, or attempt to convey the emotion of the occasion? Mr Tranter would enjoin accuracy on her. Perhaps that was what her readers would want. Not to dwell on the tragedy which had overwhelmed the family, but to mark the passing of one of them. Members of a community, inheritors of a tradition which stretched back to the medieval goldsmiths who financed the conquests of monarchs. There was a stirring at the back of the church. As she glanced round, she glimpsed Sergeant Bragg sitting by the aisle, near the font. James did not appear to be with him. Then the organ faded into silence; there was a shuffling as the congregation got to its feet. The mellifluous voice of the parson announced a hymn.

> *O God, our help in ages past,*
> *Our hope for years to come,*

The men around her were singing heartily, almost defiantly. Throwing down the gauntlet to that fate which had so untimely despatched their colleague.

60

Time, like an ever rolling stream,
Bears all its sons away:

Would they remember this, Catherine wondered, once the shock had abated; when they had returned to the daily struggle to compete, survive, eclipse their rivals?

Be thou our guard while troubles last,
And our eternal home.

As the hymn was ending, the family mourners reached the front of the nave, and filed into the empty pews. The widow was supported on the arm of an elderly man; perhaps her father. Her face was white, her lips compressed into a thin line. She was not weeping, but she looked dazed and ill. Catherine was surprised to see Gideon Wicks follow her into the pew. She instinctively turned her head, lest he should see her. How stupid! she chided herself. He would hardly recognise her, amongst this crowd. Anyway, she was here professionally; it was a City occasion.

Catherine tried to lose herself in the service, to let the sonorous language seduce her senses. But, somehow, Wicks's presence irked her. She had been spying on him only two days ago; caught up in Sergeant Bragg's fantasy, casting him in her mind as some arch-criminal. Now here he was – solicitous, protective, supportive. She tried to listen to the parson's address. In her sour mood it seemed banal and facile. She was no longer sure she wanted to spend eternity playing a harp, and chanting platitudinous praises. At last the sermon came to an end, and another hymn was announced. Catherine did not even attempt to sing it. She was watching Needham's widow; looking through her eyes as the undertaker's men filed into the chancel. With practised solemnity they took the coffin on their shoulders, and bore it slowly down the aisle. Mrs Needham stumbled, as she left the pew to follow, but Wicks supported her. Catherine told herself that she was being stupid, sentimental. But this still-young woman was following the mortal remains of her husband. Within a few minutes he would be interred, buried under six feet of clay. And she? Abandoned to a lifetime of isolation, of ostracism almost; for society had no time for widows. It was so unfair! Well, Catherine would never allow herself to be put in such a position. If she could not keep her independence within marriage, she told herself, she would happily die an old maid.

Bragg had a leisurely lunch in a pub, in Windsor High Street. Then, promptly on two o'clock, he presented himself at the National Provincial bank. On being told that the manager was lunching with a client, he elected to wait. He prowled up and down the banking hall, his irritation mounting. Now and again the clerks would glance at him reproachfully. Finally, one of them suggested that he should take a seat in the corner. The immobility, if anything, soured his temper all the more. At a quarter to three, a dapper little man entered the bank, and scurried through a door at the rear. After a further five minutes, a clerk ushered Bragg into the manager's office.

The little man rose to his feet, hand outstretched. 'I am sorry to have been at a meeting, Mr, er ... In future, it would be advisable to make an appointment.'

Bragg tossed his warrant-card on the desk. 'I don't make appointments,' he growled, sitting opposite him.

The manager nervously tugged his little moustache, peering at Bragg's card. 'Dear me!' he said in alarm. 'I cannot remotely think why the City police should be interested in us.'

'Not you. One of your customers.'

A wary look spread over the manager's face. 'I see. May I have the name of this client?' he asked.

'Clifford Needham, very much deceased.'

'Ah, yes. We have been burying him today.'

'We know that he had an account at this branch of your bank,' Bragg said. 'I want to have a quick look at your ledger.'

The manager frowned. 'What you ask is totally beyond my competence,' he said irritably.

'Why? You are in charge.'

'It ought to be perfectly obvious, even to you, sergeant. The essence of banking is confidentiality. Complete confidentiality in all circumstances.'

'I don't see that this client would care one way or another, at the moment.'

62

'But we do not know, do we? It might be the last thing that his personal representatives would wish.'

Bragg looked at him coldly. 'Are you saying Needham might have been some kind of criminal?' he asked.

'No, not at all!' the manager exclaimed in a shocked tone.

'Then, why would anyone deliberately set out to hinder the investigation into his murder?'

'There is no question of my seeking to do that,' the manager said irritably. 'But my own authority is circumscribed. I have to work within rules of conduct laid down by the bank's head office.'

'And they might decide to hinder our enquiries?'

The manager looked flustered. 'I am not saying that. I cannot conceive that they would do other than their civic duty. But it is not in my power to anticipate their decisions.'

'Are they on the telephone system?' Bragg asked. 'Let me talk to them'

The manager attempted a smile. 'The National Provincial have always been suspicious of so-called aids to efficiency.'

'So, how do you get permission to let me see his account?'

The manager looked at him warily. 'I could write to my head office, this afternoon. The letter would be on the desk of my superior by tomorrow morning.'

'Which is Friday. And when does he get around to replying?'

The manager shrugged. 'That would be up to him.'

Bragg jumped to his feet, towering over the man. 'If you think you can bugger me about, mate, you are bloody mistaken!' he growled. 'Once I report to the coroner that you are deliberately frustrating my enquiries, you might as well say goodbye to your job. He will have a court order in two shakes of a winkle's prick! Shall I tell you what will happen? We will fill this branch with detectives and accountants. You won't be able to move for them. There won't be room here for customers, until they have finished. We shall examine Needham's account then, all right. But that won't be all. Who knows but that he might have had transactions with other clients here. He came from Windsor originally. I can't think that Sir Rufus Stone would be satisfied, until we had looked at every account in the branch ... perhaps even other branches in the area. Believe me, he would subpoena the Queen, if he thought she could tell us anything!'

The manager looked dazed. He blinked his eyes rapidly, then took a deep breath. 'What is it you want?' he asked defeatedly.

'Just a quick look at Needham's account, for the moment.'

The manager pressed an electric bell on his desk, and a young clerk came in. 'Bring me the ledger containing the account of Clifford Needham,' he ordered.

They sat in angry silence until the youth came back. He set a heavy ledger on the manager's desk, and retreated deferentially. The manager opened the ledger, gestured towards his chair, and went to stare out of the window.

Bragg examined the Needham account. It had been opened in 1868. References had been obtained from the local vicar and doctor. There was a pencil note at the head of the page, to the effect that Needham's father was a local solicitor. An address in Windsor was recorded. In the early years, the transactions on the account had been simplicity itself. A cheque had been deposited each month, and weekly cash withdrawals had been made against it. The balance on the account had never exceeded eleven pounds until 1870, when there was a sizeable increase in the amount of the monthly cheque. A promotion, presumably. Thereafter the balance built up gradually, while the withdrawals remained more or less at the former level. In 1879, there was another increase in salary. Even so, the cash withdrawals remained modest. It was a bit peculiar. By now, Needham must have been in his late twenties, early thirties. A lot of money in the bank, and still living like a school-leaver.

Bragg turned the page. Hello! A change in the pattern at last! In addition to the salary cheque, there was a deposit of cash – three of them, towards the end of 1881. Had it been just one, it could conceivably have been accumulated surplus funds. But not with three ... Perhaps he had been doing work on the side. Advising someone on insurance, perhaps. That could have been a risky course; taking cash away from his firm. He could have got the sack for it. But no ... That could not be the explanation. In '82 the deposits were more frequent; and the amounts were getting bigger, too. In 1884 there was a note that Needham had married, and a different address in Windsor was recorded. Thereafter withdrawals increased in amount and frequency; now they more or less equalled the salary cheque deposits. But the unexplained credits were increasing, also.

Then, in 1886, the whole pattern altered. Regular transfers began to the Colonial bank in Bishopsgate. Both changes must have been connected with his promotion at the Imperial company, and his move to Finsbury Circus. From that point, the Colonial bank must have been where his household account was kept. And he seemed to be living above his salary. So he was relying on these other credits ... But why bother to keep the Windsor account open at all? Just sentiment? Hardly. A nest-egg his wife didn't know about? Maybe ... And the account was still being fed. There were irregular but substantial transfers of cash going into it. Against one of them a clerk had inserted a pencil note: 'N. P. Lothbury.'

Morton paused in front of the Cornhill Gallery and gazed at the furniture displayed. Miss Marsden was certainly right; there were some exquisite pieces. In terms of quality, the shop was on a par with the best in Bond Street. Then, why were its proprietors so discreet? Perhaps their connection was indeed so exclusive that they did not need to advertise. Their business might be conducted wholly by word of mouth. That was the way of the City. Here personal connections were paramount; networks of people with similar interests, business and private.

He pushed inside. The only person there was a young woman, of medium height and slender build. She was wearing a pale cream blouse and deep blue skirt. She was not a customer, or she would have worn a coat and hat. Surely Sergeant Bragg had mentioned only the proprietor, Wicks.

She gave him a bright smile, as he entered. 'Good morning,' she said, in a warm Welsh voice. 'Lovely day, isn't it?'

'Beautiful!' He began to browse around the shop, conscious that her eyes were following him; deep violet, lively eyes. She had now picked up a feather duster, and was flicking it over the polished surfaces of the furniture. Morton felt slightly irritated. It was almost as if she were keeping him under observation. But that was not wholly unreasonable. Shoplifters did operate in such stores, masquerading as customers. How was she to know that here was a policeman masquerading as a customer?

His good humour restored, he began a systematic perusal of the paintings. As Miss Marsden had said, they were an astonishing collection. He could not claim for himself any great expertise, but they certainly looked authentic. He found the Stubbs, which Bragg said had made him uneasy. The background was mainly a great, dense oak tree; dark, almost menacing. Sunlight was coming from a patch of blue sky, on the right, illuminating the subject – a man and a woman in a light carriage, their clothes bright against the foliage. The horse was a splendid grey. And, for once in a Stubbs, the head was the right size for its body, instead of being impossibly small. Could that be what had made Bragg uneasy?

'Do you like that one?' The young woman was standing at his elbow.

'Indeed I do!'

A heart-shaped locket nestled between the full swell of her breasts. Her waist was trim, her hips wide. The top of her head came just about level with his shoulder. Her body seemed to consist of a series of curves; enticing, seductive curves.

'You should have seen it before my father restored it,' she said in a laughing, lilting voice. 'It was a terrible mess! The old varnish was so brown, you could hardly make out what was under it.'

'Is your father a picture restorer?' Morton asked.

'Not by choice! He trained as a painter. He was at the Slade School of Art with Mr Wicks, who owns this gallery.'

'I see.'

'He still does some painting. But it's hard to make your way in London, if you come from the Celtic fringes.' The warmth of her smile robbed the words of any bitterness.

'And you assist Mr Wicks in the gallery?'

'Oh, no! He had to go to a funeral, see. I'm only here till he gets back – though I fear I shall get little reward for it.'

'Does he not pay you?' Morton asked.

'I shall get a commission on what I sell – which is why I am pestering you!'

Morton smiled. 'I do not feel the least bit pestered,' he said. 'You are being most charmingly informative. And, what do you do when you are not pestering people here?'

'I weave tapestries. See, that is one of mine, on the wall there.'

Morton crossed to examine it. 'But it is beautiful!' he exclaimed. 'At first sight I would have thought it was Pre-Raphaelite; but it has more strength, more individuality. It is as if its roots are in a living tradition.'

She looked up in his face and gave a teasing smile. 'You sound like an art critic,' she said.

'Only because I find it difficult to put my reactions into words.'

She smiled impishly. 'Now, if you were to buy it, you would be able to look at it until the right words came!'

Morton laughed. 'I fear it would swamp my rather small, bachelor rooms ... There might be a place for it in my parents' house. There is room enough for it, goodness knows. But my mother has very decided views on decoration. For instance, she refused to have electricity to light the great hall. In the more modern parts of the house it was allowed; but not in the monastic hall. So I dare not impose your tapestry on her, even though it would be eminently in keeping.'

She smiled. 'Oh, no. That would never do! So what can I sell you?'

'Well, actually, I was rather taken with the five-drawer chest, there; the one in the walnut oyster veneer.'

'It's beautiful! But it's expensive.'

'Then your commission will be all the greater. How much is it?'

A shadow crossed her face. 'Eighty pounds, I'm afraid.'

'Will you take a cheque? You need not deliver it until the cheque is cleared.'

She gave a delighted smile. 'I'm sure Mr Wicks would be agreeable to that.'

'Excellent! Who should I make the cheque out to?'

'Gideon Wicks ... It's such a stuffy old-fashioned name, isn't it? And he's not a bit like that!'

Morton scribbled his signature at the bottom of his cheque and handed it to her. 'And how will you spend your commission?' he asked.

She smiled intimately. 'I shall have a lovely few days just thinking about it ... What is your name? I can't read your writing!'

'Morton, James Morton.'

'And where do you want the chest delivered to?'

'Why, I suppose it ought to come to my rooms in Alderman's Walk – over the hatter's shop.'

She gave a half-smile. 'I hope you are not teasing me over this,' she said.

'Not at all,' Morton protested. 'In fact, I was wondering if I

67

could persuade your father to accept a commission from me. I promise to pay in advance!'

She put her hand on his arm. 'I'm sorry if I vexed you, with what I said. But there are some funny people about.'

Morton looked into her sparkling violet eyes. 'I doubt if I could ever become vexed with you,' he said.

She smiled then broke away. 'What is this commission for my dad?'

'You say that he studied painting at the Slade, and is now a restorer. With that background he should be ideal for my purpose ... I have an elder brother who is dying.'

A shadow of sympathy crossed her face. She laid her hand on his arm. 'That is awful,' she said. 'He can't be any age at all.'

'He is six years older than I am. And family tradition dictated that he should go into the army.'

'Family tradition?'

'My father is a general, as was his father ... Anyway, Edwin went into the cavalry, in his turn. But Lady Luck deserted him. He was hit by a Dervish bullet, in the Sudan, and brought back crippled.'

'Oh! How dreadful! When was this?'

'At the battle of Abu Kru in '85. He has been kept alive by devoted nursing, ever since. But I doubt if he can last much longer.'

'I am so sorry, James,' she said. 'But what can my dad do?'

'Well, there is a long gallery in the Elizabethan part of the house. In it are portraits of most members of my family. Certainly all the baronets are there. In the normal course, Edwin's would have appeared there too. I'm sure my parents would regret that omission for the rest of their lives. But our conversation has given me an idea.'

'Whatever is that?'

'I have a photograph of him, when he was first commissioned. Do you think that your father could create a portrait from that?'

She put her head on one side. 'I don't see why not,' she said after a moment. 'We might as well ask him, anyway.'

'Excellent! The photograph is in my rooms. How can I get it to him?'

'Why, I will give it to him ... There doesn't seem to be much happening here, this morning, anyway. I can lock up and come with you.'

They took a hansom to St Botolph's church, and walked the few yards to Morton's rooms, her hand on his arm. He ushered her up the flight of stairs. As they reached the landing, Mrs Chambers came out of the dining-room. She looked at him in surprise.

'Why, Master James, I didn't expect you back so soon,' she said in a fluster.

'That is pefectly all right, Mrs Chambers,' Morton said genially. 'This is Miss . . .' He turned and smiled at his companion. 'Do you know, I have not even asked your name,' he remarked.

'Bronwen Price,' she said with a smile.

A disapproving look crossed Mrs Chambers's face. 'Shall I leave the cleaning till later?' she asked frostily.

'Not at all, Mrs Chambers! We shall be in the drawing-room for a few moments. Come along, Bronwen!'

She followed him into a large, comfortable room, with Turkish carpets on the floor and worn leather armchairs. Over a bookcase was the portrait of a beautiful young woman, holding a rosebud pensively to her cheek.

'That's nice,' she said coolly.

Morton looked up from the bureau. 'Ah, yes. It is a Marsden.'

'William Marsden, the Academician?'

'Yes.'

'Lovely . . . Who is the sitter?' she asked casually.

'His daughter.'

Bronwen looked at it more attentively. 'You must be very close to her, to have her portrait in your rooms,' she said.

Morton laughed. 'It does not follow at all! In fact, although the painting has hung there for almost two years, she is still unaware of the fact.'

Bronwen swung round. 'Well, have you found the photograph?' she asked briskly.

'Yes, here it is.' Morton crossed over and gave it to her. 'Do you think your father could paint a portrait from that?'

She scrutinised it in the light from the window. 'We can only ask him,' she said.

'There is one difficulty,' Morton said. 'The photograph was taken some ten years ago.'

Bronwen smiled confidently. 'Oh, Dad could make him look older – plump his features out a bit.'

'Could he really?'

'Of course. Clever, my dad is . . . What colour are his eyes?'

'Brown.'

'And his complexion?'

'I suppose he had better look sunburned. We are thinking of posterity, after all.'

'I expect his hair will be brown and wavy, like yours,' she said approvingly.

'Much the same, yes.'

'I think I can remember all that! But what about the uniform? I know only the neck and shoulders will show, but we had better get it right, hadn't we?'

Morton frowned. 'I am far from sure of the detail,' he said. 'He was a captain in the Life Guards at the time he was wounded.'

'Don't worry. Dad will look it up – if he will do it, that is. Perhaps we should tell him what we are planning.'

Morton smiled. 'Then, let me escort you to your home. Where do you live?'

'We have rooms in Love Court, Whitechapel . . . Very well, so long as we walk. It's too nice to be behind a smelly horse!'

They strolled down Houndsditch, her hand in the crook of his arm, then cut across Spitalfields. Love Court was a narrow street, a few hundred yards beyond the City's boundary. It served rows of artisans' terraced houses, much like Skerret's. Bronwen stopped at a door a short way along the street, and unlocked it.

'Now, you must stay here, till I tell you to come up,' she said firmly. 'Dad may have someone modelling in the nude. We don't want to cause a scandal, do we?' She gave an arch smile and closed the door behind her. Morton waited for almost five minutes. He was beginning to think that she had been amusing herself at his expense. Then a window on the upper floor was opened, and Bronwen's head appeared.

'You can come up, now,' she said. 'Turn right at the top of the stairs.'

She met him on the landing. She had changed into a thin cotton dressing-gown that revealed the cleft of her bosom.

'Dad is out,' she said. 'But you can see some of his work, if you like.'

She led him into a studio. The only furniture was a sofa, opposite the fireplace. There were empty picture-frames stacked against the walls; one or two canvases whose pictures were virtually obscured by layers of dirt and varnish. On an easel by the window was a full-length picture of a nude woman. It was not that of a classical nymph, by any means. She was in early middle-age, but her body was lithe and smooth. She cradled her left breast in her right hand, her eyes looking challengingly at the beholder. The hair round her mount of Venus had been painted meticulously. It was brown and soft and enticing. Morton had never seen such sensuality in a painting before. This was the reality of love, it seemed to say; not a cold, marble statue of Venus. Here was tenderness and passion, softness and fierceness, striving and release.

Bronwen came close to him, her gown parted. She took his hand and placed it on her breast, her soft lips smiling. He could no longer control his carnal instincts, no longer still his clamorous desires. As they kissed, he picked her up and laid her gently on the sofa.

5

Friday morning found Morton in Bragg's room early. He had a persistent sense of disquiet over the Bronwen episode, but he put it behind him. Why not? He was unattached; she was willing and he was able ... And life was too unsure. In his work, a slight miscalculation, a moment's inattention and he could be maimed; a shattered hulk like his brother. Life was to be taken as it came ... A vision of Catherine Marsden formed in his mind; cool and condemnatory. Well, she had her own priorities, and they did not appear to include him. He took a pad, and began to jot down his impressions of the Cornhill Gallery.

Bragg came in. He hung up his coat and took out his pipe.

'How did the funeral go, sir?' Morton asked, turning round in his chair.

'Interesting. Our friend Wicks seemed to be one of the chief supporters of the widow.' Bragg struck a match, laid it across his pipe, and sucked greedily at the flame.

'I thought that she had family in Windsor,' Morton said.

'Oh, there were plenty of other mourners – from his side, too, I reckon.'

'And the ceremony passed off satisfactorily?'

'Yes, lad. And I will say this for the widow, she looked genuinely upset ... I don't know what is the matter with this pipe,' he said with a grimace. 'It tastes like camel dung!' He knocked it out, and placed in his ashtray.

'And I did have a very interesting chat with the bank manager,' he went on.

'At the National Provincial?'

'Yes. You should look through my notes, later. But the gist of them is that Needham has been living beyond his apparent means for years. Also, there were sizeable deposits of cash, beginning in '81.'

'That does seem strange,' Morton said. 'Considering that he was in employment.'

'Yes. There was something funny going on. The question is, was it connected with his murder? Anyway, how did you get on, lad?'

'As you already know, Wicks himself was not at the gallery. The person in charge was a charming young lady called Bronwen Price. Her father apparently does picture restoring for Wicks.'

Bragg snorted censoriously. 'Then, if she was so comely, I don't suppose you took much notice of anything else.'

'On the contrary! I was able to browse around for upwards of an hour. I saw your Stubbs. Bronwen's father had, in fact, restored it for Wicks. It was apparently in rather a bad state.'

'What is involved in this restoration?' Bragg asked grumpily.

'I have very little idea, sir. I know that the surface coat of varnish darkens with age. I take it that it has to be removed and replaced.'

'And what did you think of it?'

'The Stubbs? It seemed to be a run-of-the-mill conversation piece. He probably churned them out by the score.'

Bragg grunted. 'I don't know about conversation. The couple looked as if they had just had an almighty row! Not much love lost there, I reckon.'

'I have a theory about what may be the source of your disquiet,' Morton said with a grin.

'Go on, then.'

'In most of the Stubbs paintings one sees, the subject is a racehorse. Usually they have an Arab blood-line, and thus, smaller heads than European bloodstock.'

'Huh!' Bragg interrupted. 'There was never a horse alive that looked like some of his. I've seen better rocking-horses.'

'Be that as it may, in the Cornhill Gallery painting, the head of the horse is of more or less normal proportions. Presumably because it was a carriage horse.'

'Oh, well,' Bragg said grudgingly. 'Perhaps you are right. What about the whole set-up there?'

'I agree with Miss Marsden, that the stock is of very high quality. There were many items that I coveted myself.'

'So, whoever owns it – Wicks, I presume – has had to lay out a dollop of money to set it up ... What do you think the profit margin would be, on that class of stuff?'

Morton pursed his lips. 'It must depend on how well you can buy ... I suppose the mark-up might be one-third on cost, at the very least. After all, the overheads are constant; sales may be irregular.'

'Hmm ... Would he own the shop, do you think?'

'I doubt it. Certainly not the freehold. On that side of Cornhill, the ground landlords are the Merchant Taylors' Company.'

Bragg knocked out his pipe. 'Then let's have a word with them.'

They strolled in fitful sunshine down Threadneedle Street, and turned down the alley that led to the Merchant Taylors' hall. It was imposing in its grandeur, as befitted the largest of the twelve great livery companies. The doorman was disdainful, on discovering that the visitors were mere policemen. But eventually they found themselves in a rather shabby office in the depths of the building. A clerk stood as they entered.

'I gather that you are enquiring about our property holdings,' he said amiably.

'That's right, sir,' Bragg said taking a chair opposite him. 'I believe you own the freehold of the land to the south of Cornhill and immediately east of the Bank junction.'

'Indeed we do, officer; to as far as Gracechurch Street to the east.'

'Good. Can you tell us who you have it leased to?'

'Of course.' He crossed to a wooden press and took out a large ledger. He turned the pages. 'Ah, here we are ... yes, the whole of the triangular block bordered by Cornhill, Gracechurch Street and Lombard Street is currently leased to the Turbridy Estate.'

'That would be a long lease, I take it,' Bragg said.

'Yes, indeed! I see that a lease for ninety-nine years was taken up by Alderman George Turbridy in 1857. He is, of course, long departed this life!'

'So, who is dealing with it now?'

The man looked back at the ledger. 'Such correspondence as we have is conducted with a firm of solicitors – Wellbeloved & Co., in Chancery Lane.'

'Thank you, sir. Then, we had better go to see them.'

Now it was mid-morning, and every cab in sight was already

occupied. They had trudged past St Paul's Cathedral, and half-way along Fleet Street, before they saw an empty hansom. By then Bragg was in a thoroughly peevish mood. He refused to spend good money for a cab to take him only a few hundred yards, even if he could claim it back. So they plodded on. Then they had to climb two flights of steep stairs to the offices of Wellbeloved & Co. Bragg's spirits were lightened somewhat by the smiling face of the young woman who greeted them.

'Can I help you?' she asked cheerfully.

'City police.' Bragg showed her his warrant-card. 'We would like a quick word with whoever deals with the Turbridy Estate.'

Her face clouded. 'I have never heard of that client,' she said. 'But I will ask the chief clerk. Do sit down for a moment.'

They waited for several minutes before a grey-haired man in a morning coat approached them. 'You were asking about the Turbridy Estate,' he said.

'That is right, sir,' Bragg said amiably.

'And you are City police officers.'

'Yes.' Bragg made to produce his warrant-card, but the clerk held up his hand.

'I believe you conducted the formalities with Miss Pleasance,' he said with a smile. 'Would you come this way?'

He led them to a cramped office at the back of the building, with a view over the rooftops to St Paul's.

'We want a quick word about the assets of the estate, sir,' Bragg said, taking the proffered chair. 'We understand that the Turbridy Estate holds a ninety-nine-year lease on a block at the west end of Cornhill.'

The clerk wrinkled his brow. 'That is the case,' he said.

'I take it that the land has been sub-let.'

'Rather, the Turbridy Estate erected buildings on the land, and leased them.' He went to a press, and came back with a bulky file. 'Are you concerned to enquire about the whole block, or a specific part of it?' he asked.

'Twelve, Cornhill.'

'Ah! The sharp end.' The man began to turn through a pile of sub-files. 'Here we are! The estate has granted a series of short leases, normally for five years. The last one on number twelve began on the first of January this year.'

'1895?' Bragg asked in surprise. 'But that is only three months ago! The concern we are interested in, has been operating for longer than that.'

The clerk shrugged. 'It is possible that the trader purchased the unexpired period of the previous lease. The estate would not object to that.'

'So, who holds the present lease of number twelve?'

'A company named George Barber Ltd.'

'A company?' Bragg said in surprise.

'Indeed, sergeant. And I see, from a note here, that it also leases from us a small warehouse at eight, Crooked Lane – that is by King William's statue.'

'And is that company active, sir? I mean, do you have regular dealings with it?'

The clerk turned over the papers in the sub-file. 'No,' he said at length. 'It would be true to say that, after the signing of the lease, we have had no contact with the company whatever. I see that the rent is paid quarterly, by a firm of solicitors.'

'And who would they be?'

'Jarvis, Gittings & Crump, of Lincoln's Inn.'

Bragg sighed. 'I am most grateful to you, sir,' he said. 'Thank you.'

'These buggers can sew it up as tight as a sheep's arsehole,' Bragg exclaimed bitterly, when they reached the street. 'Pay a string of lawyers to screen you, and you can do what the hell you like.'

'We can scarcely complain,' Morton said with a smile. 'In our turn, we are proceeding on an assumption that is scarcely warranted by the facts so far ascertained.'

'But we are paid to get at the truth, lad! To shake these sods until it drops out.'

'We are hardly likely to find Jarvis, Gittings & Crump particularly forthcoming, unless their client allows it.'

'No. But some things are in the public domain. Since we are so far west, we might as well go a bit further.'

This time they managed to stop a passing hansom. It deposited them in the Strand, outside Somerset House. Bragg marched through the courtyard, to the office of the Registrar of Joint Stock Companies. He banged a bell on the public counter, until a clerk appeared. He had a tired air and drooping moustache.

'Police,' Bragg said crisply, waving his warrant-card. 'I want the file of George Barber Ltd.'

The man was unimpressed. 'You got the register number?' he asked.

'No.'

'Do you know what date it was registered?'

'No.'

'Looks like you know bugger all!' the clerk complained.

'We do know,' Morton intervened, 'that it was in existence by the beginning of this year, because it entered into a rental agreement in January.'

'That's not much to go on. I shall have to go right through the index . . . Can't you come back some other time?'

'No, we bloody can't!' Bragg growled. 'Get on with it!'

The man went through a door at the back, and the policemen were left to cool their heels. From time to time members of the public came in, mainly solicitors' clerks. They generally had the magical registration number. In a matter of moments a clerk would produce a file; they would glance at it briefly, make a few notes, and be on their way. As the minutes ticked by, Bragg's irritation mounted. Morton half expected him to throw himself over the counter, march into the mysterious depths of the filing room beyond, and fetch the clerk out by the scruff of his neck. After twenty minutes had elapsed, the man finally appeared. He flung a thin file on the counter in front of them.

'Next time, make sure you have the number,' he said peevishly.

Bragg said nothing. He picked up the file and opened it. George Barber Ltd had been registered barely six months. The registration documents had been submitted by Sanderson & Co., of High Holborn. According to the file, the registered office was still at that address. Bragg jotted down the relevant details in his note-book, then closed the file.

'Thank you for your assistance, sir,' he said with heavy irony, then marched outside.

'What now, sir?' Morton asked, when they regained the street.

'I'm not giving up, till I have tried everything,' Bragg growled. 'Get that cab, lad!'

By now the traffic was building up. Their hansom seemed to spend more time stationary than moving. It seemed to Morton that they were likely to reach their destination, only to find that the staff had departed for lunch. Then their driver pulled off the main road and, by dint of zigzagging through a maze of side-streets, deposited them in High Holborn. They found the offices of Sanderson & Co., and went in. A smart young woman was sitting at a reception desk. She looked up as they entered, and smiled.

'Police!' Bragg produced his warrant-card. 'I want a quick word about a company you set up,' he said.

She looked at him hesitantly. 'Perhaps you ought to speak to Mr Alton,' she said. 'Just one moment.'

She was gone for several minutes, and Bragg took to prowling about restively. Then a balding, weasel-faced man appeared.

'What is it you want?' he asked sharply.

'Sanderson & Co. set up a new company, last December,' Bragg said. 'It was called George Barber Ltd.'

'What about it?'

'I want to know who owns it.'

The man frowned. 'How should I know?' he said belligerently. 'We set up scores, every month. We are company promoters. We turn them over as quickly as we can.'

'According to the Company Registrars, the registered office is still at this address. The seven subscribing shareholders have given their addresses as these premises.'

'It is up to the purchasers of the issued capital to notify the change of registered office,' the man said sharply. 'Read the Companies Act. Once the shares in a company are sold, we have no further responsibility for it.'

'That's a queer state of affairs, sir,' Bragg said darkly. 'You can set up a company, then wash your hands of it completely?'

'That is the law, officer. It is the purchasers who are in default, not us. If you gave the matter a moment's thought, you would see that the individuals who bought the shares from us, could have been mere nominees of the true purchaser. Our possession of their names would help no one.'

'Hmm . . . Nevertheless, I would like you to check your records, sir, if you would be so good.'

A rebellious look flitted across the man's face, then he turned on his heel and went out. Minutes passed, Bragg getting more and more restive. Then the man appeared with a ledger in his hand. He opened it and pointed to an entry.

'There you are,' he said. 'George Barber Ltd. Registered on the fourteenth of October, last year. The subscribing shareholders, there, are employees of my business. They sold their shares, on the twenty-seventh of that month, as an element of the purchase price.'

'How much would that be?'

'In this case, fifty pounds.'

Bragg whistled. 'You get as much as that, just for filling up a few forms?' he exclaimed.

'It is the going rate,' the man said brusquely.

'And, who bought the company?'

The man clapped the ledger shut. 'I have no idea, officer,' he said. 'The fifty pounds was paid in cash.'

Catherine followed the maid, with some trepidation, into the sitting-room of the Needhams' house.

'It is so good of you to see me, Mrs Needham,' she said warmly. 'I know this is a dreadful time for you. But our readers have been greatly disturbed by your husband's death. They regard the obituary as utterly inadequate to mark his contribution to the life of the City.'

Mrs Needham motioned Catherine to a chair. Her auburn hair gave her a Pre-Raphaelite look. She had a cool, classical beauty, belied by a tip-tilted nose. 'I am seeing you because Clifford would have wished it,' she said. Her face was drawn, she looked weary; but it did not appear that she had cried much.

Catherine took out her notebook and pencil. 'My editor accepts that scant justice has been done to Mr Needham; that more is due to his memory than a bare recital of the posts he has held in the City. So the idea is that I should do a more general article, for tomorrow's edition; in a sense, to celebrate his life.'

A slight smile touched Mrs Needham's lips. 'I am sure he would have wanted me to co-operate with you,' she said.

'And, of course, you have experienced the most dreadful loss that any woman can face in life. Our female readers will be putting themselves in your place, wondering how they would be able to cope with such a tragedy; sharing to that extent in your grief.'

An embarrassed look crossed Mrs Needham's face, and Catherine resolved to make her approach more businesslike. 'I gather that you were brought up together, in Windsor,' she said.

'In the sense that our families lived in the same neighbourhood, yes.'

'Was your father in a profession also?'

'Yes. He is an accountant, whereas my father-in-law is a solicitor.'

'Professionally speaking, an ideal marriage,' Catherine said, in an attempt to lighten the atmosphere.

Mrs Needham did not reply.

'Would you like to tell our readers how you met your husband?' Catherine asked gently.

'Met him? I cannot really say how or when I met him. He was always there, in the background. He was a friend of my eldest brother.'

'He was obviously older than you, by some years.'

'By almost fifteen years.'

'Do you regret that?'

Mrs Needham looked up sharply. 'That is a strange question,' she said irritably. 'It was a matter of being able to live a secure and comfortable life. My family was not wealthy. The practice had to support not only my father, but two of my brothers also. There was no question of a dowry, so my choice was limited.'

'Would you support the movement which advocates that girls should have exactly the same opportunities in life as boys?' Catherine asked quietly.

'In principle, of course. But, as to how it would work out in practice, I am not sure.'

Catherine let a pause develop, then: 'What is your first memory of your late husband?' she asked.

Mrs Needham gazed out of the window, her brow furrowed. 'I suppose it must have been when I was four. I remember his coming to play croquet with my brother, on a brilliant summer's day; though most of my recollection has been formed by my late husband's account of the occasion. He and my brother had just left their respective schools, and were celebrating their entry into adult life.'

'What school did Mr Needham attend?'

'St Jude's, at Malmesbury. It was originally a foundation for the sons of Church of England clergymen; but perforce had to draw most of its pupils from a wider class.'

'I gather that he took up a post with the Imperial Fire Insurance Company, immediately on leaving school. Presumably he would have travelled up to the City daily.'

'Yes. He did so until nine years ago.'

'And you were married when?'

'In 1884, when he was thirty-four and I was twenty.'

'Conventional wisdom would have it that such an age difference is ideal,' Catherine remarked.

'Perhaps,' Mrs Needham said flatly. 'As you can imagine, I was given comfortable surroundings, ample money to satisfy my needs. Most women would have envied me, until now.'

'So, you did not always live here,' Catherine prompted her gently.

'No. We began married life in a small house in Windsor. Of course, I was still close to my family and friends. But I saw very little of Clifford, during the week. And by Saturday afternoon he was exhausted. It took him until Monday morning to recuperate his energies ... In some ways I was more lonely than before my marriage. By then my friends were immersed in their own lives, with husbands and homes. Believe me, Miss Marsden, there are limits to the satisfaction one can derive from embroidery.'

'Did you not have children yourself?' Catherine asked quietly.

'No. That side of our marriage was a disappointment to me. I had no idea what to expect; but I did not anticipate near-indifference.'

Catherine sensed that she was on dangerous ground, and switched her line of questioning. 'I suppose your life changed radically, when you came to live here,' she said. 'When was that?'

'In 1886. My husband's promotion meant that he was regularly working late. He was compelled to stay at his club for two or three nights a week. During the summer, I was able to fill my time pleasurably in Windsor. But the winters left me feeling isolated. So I persuaded him to agree to our living in town ... I confess that I had imagined an apartment in the West End, where I would have friends all around me. I could foresee us going to concerts, becoming a modest part of the social whirl. But, instead, he took a lease on this house ... Incredibly, I found myself more isolated than before. My neighbours are not congenial; and one cannot make a friend of a servant. The highlight of my existence has become the weekly visit that I pay to my parents.'

Catherine paused, then: 'How will you manage, now that you have been widowed?' she asked.

Mrs Needham frowned. 'As you can imagine, because of the age difference I have always had to contemplate the possibility of a long widowhood. Clifford has taken out large life insurance policies. He assured me that I would be able to live comfortably.'

'That, at least, is a blessing.' Catherine closed her shorthand-pad and slipped it into her bag.

'And how do you come to be working as a journalist?' Mrs Needham asked. 'I thought it was still a man's domain.'

Catherine smiled. 'I suppose it is, so far as newspapers are concerned ... If I am honest, I got my post through influence – though, as it was my father's influence, I feel it was legitimate!'

'I see. And what was the nature of this influence? Does he own part of the concern that publishes the *City Press*?'

'By no means! He is William Marsden, the painter. I suspect that he must have painted a more than usually flattering portrait of the owner's wife! However that may be, I persuade myself that I hold my job by reason of my own ability.'

'I must say that I admire you,' Mrs Needham said enviously. 'But you must have had a better education than I received.'

'I went to Cheltenham Ladies' College which, I like to think, gave me as rigorous an education as any boys' public school.'

Mrs Needham sighed. 'In my family, education for girls was regarded as superfluous, if not downright dangerous ... And will you marry, or follow your career?'

Catherine smiled. 'Both, I hope.'

'I very much envy you your capacity to choose,' Mrs Needham said regretfully.

Catherine got to her feet 'I am most grateful to you, Mrs Needham, for giving me this interview,' she said. 'I am sure it will be well received.'

'It will be in tomorrow's edition?'

'Yes.' Catherine looked across at the painting over the escritoire. 'What a beautiful scene,' she said. 'Is it a Constable?'

'Yes. It is a prospect of Dedham Vale – one of several, I understand.'

'It must be very valuable.'

Mrs Needhan gave a thin smile. 'I hope I am never in the position of having to find out how valuable,' she said.

Bragg and Morton called for Skerret at eleven o'clock that night. They walked back to the City through shadowy, gas-lit alleys; working their way towards Crooked Lane. Number eight was a low warehouse, which had been erected at the rear of a much larger building, fronting on King William Street. They stood on a corner until they saw the beat constable appear. He walked with measured tread down one side of the lane, trying the doors as he went. Bragg had a mounting fear that he might find one broken open, would sound an alarm, bring men from neighbouring beats clattering over. But no. He tramped stolidly on until he was out of sight.

'Right,' Bragg whispered. 'According to the beat card, we have half an hour before he comes down here again. So we must hurry.'

They crossed to the double doors of number eight. Bragg and Morton stood screening Skerret while he manipulated his pick-locks. There came a click, and he gave a sigh of satisfaction.

'I hope you don't tell nobody I done this for you, Mr Bragg,' he said. 'Wouldn't go down well with my lot.'

'Nor with mine, if we're caught,' Bragg said grimly. 'In we go!'

The beams from their acetylene torches illuminated a jumble of furniture, clocks, mirrors, even a silver candelabrum placed on a table.

'Don't disturb dust, if you can help it,' Bragg said. 'I just want an idea of the kind of stuff that is here.'

Morton picked his way towards the rear of the warehouse. One or two items had been covered with dust-sheets. Perhaps because they were more valuable than the rest ... By the outline of that one, it must be a long-case clock. He carefully removed the sheet. Yes, indeed! A most handsome piece. He shone his torch at the dial. Made by William Smith, of London. And here was the maker's number – 5708. He must remember that. He heard Bragg's anxious summons. He gently replaced the dust-sheet, and crept back to the door.

Once outside, Tommy Skerret relocked the door and hurried away to the safety of Stepney. Bragg and Morton strolled to Eastcheap and went into a pub. Morton wrinkled his nose with distaste at the smoke-laden fug; but Bragg did not seem to notice it. He came back to the table with foaming glasses of beer. He drank deeply, and sighed with satisfaction.

'Well, lad, what do you think about that?' he asked, wiping the foam from his ragged moustache with the back of his hand.

'There are undoubtedly some very fine pieces there,' Morton replied. 'Much too valuable to be allowed to accumulate dust in that way.'

'Hmm ... Of course, we do not actually know it has anything to do with the Cornhill Gallery place. This George Barber company may have sub-let the store and the shop to different people.'

Morton smiled. 'But you hope not,' he said.

'Well, let's say this. For the moment we will keep an open mind.'

'Or try to!'

Bragg sniffed. 'Yes. Or try to.'

6

Catherine strolled on her father's arm along Cornhill, next morning. He had demurred at first. He was a creative artist, not a critic, he complained. Moreover, he had no wish to become involved in giving expert evidence in courts of law. Far better to approach some lecturer at one of the art schools. Opinions were their stock-in-trade; they would seize any opportunity to promote their public standing. But she had pleaded with him; said that a scoop would enhance her standing as a journalist. And he had to admit that he had encouraged her in her career. So here he was, embroiled in subterfuge. And all, apparently, because a sergeant of police felt uneasy. Stated thus baldly, the enterprise was an absurdity. But, over the years, he had come to respect from afar the instincts of Sergeant Bragg. In any case, he never worked on a Saturday morning. And he was proud to be walking along a sunlit street, with his beautiful daughter on his arm.

'Now, remember, Papa,' Catherine said urgently. 'I told the proprietor that I was to be married. Do try to play the pleased parent!'

Mr Marsden smiled ruefully. 'I would be positively transported with delight, if it were true, I assure you!' he said.

They went into the Cornhill Gallery. Wicks smiled as they entered. 'You are the young lady who is to be married,' he said ingratiatingly.

'Yes, indeed! This is my father.'

'Then, please take your time. If you have any questions, I shall be somewhere in the gallery.'

'Thank you.'

'And, as I think I said the other day, if you are looking for a particular piece, I could probably get it for you.'

'Actually,' Catherine said, 'I was very struck with the five-drawer chest.'

'The eighteenth-century one, in walnut oyster veneers?'

'Yes! I am convinced that my father is going to buy it for me!'

'Am I really?' Mr Marsden asked indulgently.

'Yes, really, Papa! There it is, at the back. By that settee.'

Wicks cleared his throat deferentially. 'I am afraid, madam, that the chest has already been sold.'

'Sold?' Catherine exclaimed, in disappointment. 'To whom?'

'I am afraid that I could not possibly reveal the name of the purchaser, madam.'

Mr Marsden intervened. 'Well, thank them from me,' he said. 'They have saved me a great deal of money!'

'I will do my best to get you a similar one,' Wicks said. 'Could I have your name and address?'

Catherine looked crestfallen. 'I . . . No. I work in the City. I can call in from time to time.'

The fact that this prospective customer had to work for her living seemed to dampen Wicks's interest. He murmured his aquiescence, and drifted over to some other browsers.

'I will examine the paintings,' Mr Marsden said. 'It is what I came for, after all. Perhaps you should look around more generally.'

Catherine absorbed herself in the displays of furniture, china and glass, while her father strolled over to the pictures. She had been right, he thought. If they were genuine, they would be worth a fortune. He stood in front of the Constable. There was no doubt it was a splendid composition; full of vigour tempered by pastoral serenity. The physical effort involved in such a painting must have been immense – to say nothing of the preparatory studies.

Wicks appeared at his elbow. 'Fine, is it not? ' he murmured.

'Yes. I like pictures,' Mr Marsden said. 'How much are you asking for that one?'

'A thousand guineas.'

'That is a very great price for a picture.'

'But then,' Wicks said, with a trace of contempt in his tone, 'it has the merit of being a very large painting.' He drifted away.

Mr Marsden spent some time looking at the Gainsborough, the Stubbs and the Reynolds portraits, then he sought out Catherine.

'Remember,' he said genially, 'that you must be at your dress-maker's by half-past eleven.'

Catherine feigned surprise. 'Oh, my goodness!' she exclaimed. 'We shall have to hurry!'

Wicks noted their going, from the rear of the shop, but made no move towards them.

'Well, Papa?' Catherine asked, as they were strolling away. 'Was it as interesting as I promised?'

'Why, yes . . . I do believe it was.'

'Tell me what you found!'

Mr Marsden smiled. 'As an expert witness?' he asked.

'Yes!'

'Ah! Then, you will have to wait until I have clarified my ideas, in my own mind. And you really do have a dressmaker to go to!'

Bragg put his dead pipe in the ashtray, and stared out of his office window. Saturday was a nothing of a day, so far as work was concerned. Nobody wanted to get involved in anything, in case it might encroach on their afternoon off. So it had become a time for tidying up bits and pieces; popping off to the pub, to celebrate success or commiserate in failure. The very thought made his throat feel dry. He had almost convinced himself that he could achieve nothing worthwhile, when the door banged open and Inspector Cotton marched in. He looked about him.

'Where's your monkey, organ-grinder?' he asked sarcastically.

'Constable Morton, you mean?'

'Who else? That bugger might as well be supernumerary, for all the good he is.'

'At the moment, he is down in Harp Lane.'

'What the hell for?'

'That break-in at the furniture repository. As you will appreci-ate, sir, the owners have precious little notion of what is in their store. So it's a matter of checking each pile of furniture against their lists.'

'That will bloody take forever!'

'Yes, sir,' Bragg said stolidly. 'But, until we find that something has been stolen, we have no crime.'

'No crime? Some bugger broke in, didn't he?'

'Apparently it is not a crime merely to climb into premises. You have got to have a theft from there, as well.'

'Who says so?' Cotton asked truculently.

'Well, it's in *Wigram*, for a start. Anyway, Sir Rufus Stone confirmed it.'

The inspector's face darkened. 'Huh! That sod! But he won't come after me again!' He flung a file on Bragg's desk. 'Anyway, there is bugger all in the Needham case. Just a bludger with a bent sense of humour. You are welcome to it. You can take that box of junk back from Jackman, too. Close the bloody thing down, as soon as you can!' Cotton turned on his heel and banged the door after him.

Morton found the premises of William Smith, clock makers to the gentry, in Clerkenwell. He wondered sardonically with what fanfare they would have proclaimed the sale of one of their clocks to royalty! Since it was a Saturday morning, the proprietor of the factory was not there. So Morton had to settle for the manager. He was an elderly cockney, whose accent had been but little tamed by the onset of responsibility.

'A copper, eh?' he remarked. 'What's up, then?'

'Nothing related to your business, I assure you, sir,' Morton said. 'I am merely seeking information.'

'About what?'

'About a specific clock, made here. The number on the dial is 5708.'

'Right. Let's see what we can find. Come with me.'

He led the way through a large workshop, where clock-cases as tall as Morton himself were in process of completion. They looked like elaborate coffins propped against the wall.

'I expected to see lathes and drilling machines,' Morton remarked.

'You would have, once upon a time,' the manager said. 'But nowadays the clockwork is made in Birmingham.'

'Why is that?' Morton asked.

'Well, we don't make enough clocks for it to be worthwhile to do it ourselves any more. It's all machines now, you see, not proper craftsmanship. In the old days, it could take four months to make a complicated movement by hand. Nobody will wait that long, even if they could afford the price. It's all rush, nowadays. When I started here, we used to make for the best families in the land; to their own design, as well. I remember one long-case clock we made for an old geezer. He'd been an officer in Wellington's army; fought at Waterloo. Instead of the usual knobs and scrolls on top of the case, he had flags and cannons and such. Blimey! I wouldn't have wanted to dust it – but it looked a treat!'

'What can you tell me about the clock I am interested in?' Morton asked. 'Does that number still have any relevance?'

'Oh, yes. We still have our own set of numbers, engraved on the dial. Now, where did I put that book?' He eventually unearthed a scarred leather-bound ledger. 'Here we are,' he said, slowly turning the pages. 'Yes ... That clock was made for a Mr Fulton, in 1887.'

'Eight years ago. Excellent! Have you an address for him?'

'Yes, Chilcomb House, Chilcomb, Winchester.'

'Splendid! I am most grateful, sir. And, can you tell me its value?'

The man screwed up his face. 'I don't know what it would fetch second-hand,' he said. 'But it must have been one of our specials. It cost them all of three hundred pounds.'

Morton hurried to the nearest telephone call-office, and rang the number at Catherine's home. He knew that one of her aunts lived at Winchester, and wanted to find out if Mrs Marsden had any knowledge of the Fultons. Once the problem was explained to her, Catherine took charge of the whole enterprise. She knew perfectly well that her aunt was in residence at their Winchester house; and was convinced that they would welcome guests at Sunday luncheon. Moreover, she had remembered that Chilcomb was not far from the city. She would send a telegraph, she said. If he heard nothing further from her, he was to present himself at her home, next morning, at ten o'clock.

Having heard nothing, Morton went to Catherine's family home in Park Lane, at the appointed hour. It was a magnificent villa, with a view over Hyde Park. William Marsden had been talented but poor. In his early twenties he had earned his living by painting prospects of country estates for their proud owners. He had visited Winchester, had painted a rambling, creeper-clad mansion, and fallen in love with a daughter of the house. They had lived in a cottage, near Winchester, in the early years of their marriage. Then William had taken the plunge, and come to London. At first, Mrs Marsden had worked in a milliner's shop. Moreover she declared that she had enjoyed the experience. Then William had begun to have paintings hung in the Royal Academy exhibitions. And his celebrated portrait of Lady Lanesborough had brought society clamouring to his studio. Now he was at the pinnacle of his profession. He clearly relished the fruits of his success, but was detached enough to accept that his fame might be transient.

Morton's ring was answered by a maid in a trim uniform.

'Are you wanting Miss Catherine?' she asked.

'Yes indeed.'

'I was told to put you in the drawing-room.' She gave a knowing smile, and led him upstairs.

Morton was tempted to go out on the balcony, to watch the early strollers in Hyde Park. But it might seem that he was taking a liberty. Instead he picked up a magazine from the table. He heard the door open behind him, and felt a surge of elation.

'Good morning, James.' It was not Catherine, but her father. 'Congratulations on a successful tour of Australia.' Mr Marsden's tone was affable, without being warm.

'Thank you, sir,' Morton said.

'I gather that my daughter will not be ready to leave for some little time. So I thought I would seize the flying moment...' He took a chair opposite Morton. 'Yesterday,' he said, 'Catherine duly hauled me off to the Cornhill Gallery. And I confess that I found the whole experience intriguing. The creator of a painting has little notion of the art world beyond his studio walls. It was a salutary experience, I can tell you!'

'It is good of you to spare us the time, sir,' Morton said.

'Nonsense! I enjoyed it. Of course, I went incognito. Our pretext was that Catherine is about to be married, and I am to have the dubious honour of providing an exceptional piece of furniture for her new home. I must say that I enjoyed the experience. I would have enjoyed it even more, if the pretext had been the truth.' He looked challengingly at Morton, but got no response.

'Were you able to examine the paintings, sir?' Morton asked.

'Indeed I was. And interesting I found them. From the prices being asked, one might suppose that the proprietor is convinced of their authenticity.'

'But you have your doubts?'

'Well, utter certainty is the refuge of fools, in the art world. Without their provenance, who would say that Titian's "Pieta" was by the same hand as his "Venus of Urbino"? But, shall we say that I have great reservations.'

'What are they?'

Mr Marsden smiled expansively. 'Let us take the Constable, for instance. "A Prospect of Dedham Vale". Now, he is known to have painted several such landscapes, over his long life. Some of them are, by now, in museums and galleries. But there is nothing inherently improbable in one turning up now. Again, he seldom signed a painting. Sometimes you will find a "J. Constable pinxit" label on the back of the canvas. On the other hand, there are many Constable paintings which have immaculate provenance, yet neither signature nor label.'

'I see.'

'Then again, James, before committing himself to a final version of a large canvas, Constable would make preparatory studies. These sometimes find their way on to the market. His study for "The Leaping Horse" is a case in point. You can see it exhibited at the Victoria and Albert Museum.'

'Is there no definitive list of his works?' Morton asked in surprise.

'No. And the position is even worse, in the case of his fellow East Anglian, Gainsborough ... It is amusing to contemplate our contemporary painters going to East Anglia for the light, when what they lack is inspiration and technique!'

'There is no canon of Gainsborough's work either?' Morton asked.

'No, James. And he painted more than two hundred landscapes, in his lifetime. During that period his technique must have developed, his perceptions changed.'

'So the certainties of the commercial art market are an illusion?' Morton said.

'Rather, profitable self-delusion on the part of dealers. It is a dishonest trade. I am glad that, as a portraitist, I am not likely to become a part of it.'

'So, where does that leave us, sir?'

'Not totally without resource, James, I assure you.' Mr Marsden gave a conspiratorial smile. 'Let us agree that the manufacture of works in the style of artists such as Constable, Gainsborough and Reynolds could be a highly profitable activity. Now, how does a forger set about it? Firstly, he buys an old picture of about the right date. He cleans off the existing painting, and thus has an authentic canvas of the period. It is then a question of acquiring the colours and compositions of paint which were used at that time.'

'Would that be difficult?'

'No, James. In terms of the artists we are discussing, it would be simple enough.'

'Are you saying, sir, that one cannot confidently assert the authenticity of a painting, unless one can trace it back to the artist's easel?' Morton asked.

Mr Marsden smiled. 'Not quite. It is almost impossible – I would even say quite impossible – for a forger to successfully imitate the technique of a painter. And one's technique, if it evolves at all, does so imperceptibly. Now, take Gainsborough – pre-eminently the painter of the Age of Elegance. The detail of his paintings is exquisite. He caresses his canvas; the picture is built up with precise, delicate brush-strokes. If you look across the surface of a Gainsborough painting, it is as smooth as satin. In contrast, Constable wrestled with his subjects. His style is rougher. Individual leaves are blobs of paint, rather than brush-strokes. Look across the surface of, say, "The Hay Wain"; the finish is coarse, like tapestry.'

'So the Cornhill Gallery paintings are forgeries?' Morton asked, excitement in his voice.

'If you mean by the word that they were not painted by the masters themselves, then yes. But they are splendid pictures, nevertheless.'

'But they must have been done many years ago,' Morton said. 'Their surfaces are cracked with age.'

Mr Marsden smiled. 'I am told that, with the right ground, it is possible to achieve such an effect quite speedily. I have also heard of ageing being achieved by putting the painting into a gas oven!'

'So those pictures could have been painted recently?'

'It is entirely possible.'

'That is most helpful, sir. Thank you.'

A silence fell. Mr Marsden looked at the clock, then cleared his throat. 'As the opportunity has presented itself, James,' he said firmly, 'I feel it is my duty to ask what your intentions are towards my daughter.'

Morton looked up in surprise. 'I would not dare to have anything so presumptuous as intentions, sir,' he said lightly. 'Aspirations, perhaps; but no more.'

'You must appreciate, nevertheless, that I have certain responsibilities towards her. I suggest that the nature of her relationship with you is damaging to her prospects.'

Morton frowned. 'I must point out, sir, that her relationship with me is purely voluntary,' he said.

'I am sure that both those words indeed apply,' Mr Marsden said stiffly. 'Nevertheless, as you undoubtedly realise, in her stratum of society the way forward for a young woman is through marriage.'

'But not, I presume, to a police constable,' Morton said with a touch of flippancy. 'Undoubtedly she is beautiful and talented. The drawing-rooms of the highest in the land are open to her. She is an acquaintance of the Prince of Wales – though I believe not more than that.'

'I will have you know that my daughter is above reproach!' Mr Marsden said angrily.

'We are undoubtedly agreed on that, sir.'

'Well, then,' Mr Marsden said, with a puzzled frown, 'if you have formed an attachment to my daughter, is it your intention that it should progress to a satisfactory conclusion?'

'I would hardly call it an attachment,' Morton said. 'I am a mere comet in her firmament. I admire her from afar.'

Mr Marsden frowned. 'That cannot be so,' he said. 'She entertains no other suitors; she has refused to consider proposals of marriage from peers of the realm, no less. Her only enduring relationship is with you. And, knowing my daughter as I do, that must be significant.'

Morton smiled ruefully. 'So I have told myself, sir; though with lessening conviction.'

'Well, it cannot go on like this!'

'Perhaps not. Yet I dare not try to force a decision. When I did propose marriage to her, she saw me off in no uncertain terms.'

'You have proposed to her?' Mr Marsden said in astonishment. 'Why did she not inform me?'

'Perhaps because she feels capable of making up her own mind on the subject.'

'May I ask when you made your proposal?'

'Over a year ago,' Morton said. 'After the suicide of her friend Louisa Sommers. It was not made on an auspicious occasion, but it was nevertheless genuine.'

'Then you are not playing with her affections!'

'Rather the reverse, sir. I have begun to feel that I am no more than a useful social prop, in the drama of women's emancipation. I did think, when she was so unjustly passed over for the editorship of *The Lady*, that her resolve might falter. If anything, it seems to have made her the more determined to succeed.'

Mr Marsden sighed. 'I sometimes feel it was a great mistake to send her to Cheltenham Ladies' College,' he said. 'It has made her too independent. And she was already strong-minded enough, goodness knows.'

'I could hardly have the temerity to agree with you, sir,' Morton said with a rueful smile. 'She is utterly right in wanting to throw off the shackles of the past. I would not wish that she were other than she is. If anything, it is I who am a prisoner of the past.'

Mr Marsden frowned. 'Well, you obviously regard yourself as a suitor, if not a favoured one. Perhaps I ought to take this opportunity to enquire into your circumstances.'

Morton smiled. 'As I am sure you know from Debrett, I am the second son of Sir Henry Morton.'

'Of course. Your elder brother was wounded, in the Sudan, was he not?'

'Yes, sir,' Morton said sombrely. 'I fear that he can barely survive the year out.'

'Hmm ... Which would mean that you would inherit the baronetcy, in due course.'

'Yes.'

'And the family estates would come to you?'

'That is so.'

Mr Marsden pondered. 'Of course, that would not necessarily mean a secure future, in these days of agricultural depression.

Particularly as the Canadian corn lands are being exploited now.'

'You need have no fear, sir,' Morton said. 'My mother was the daughter of the American Ambassador here. The Harmans have extensive coal and steel interests throughout America. My grandfather set up trusts for each of his grandchildren. My trust generates a very considerable income, which I largely allow to accumulate. And I should tell you that the trust capital would vest in me, absolutely, on my marriage.'

Mr Marsden smiled warmly. 'That seems to constitute a very powerful incentive to marry,' he said.

'But only to the right person.'

'And you believe Catherine to be that person?'

'So far, sir, I have not met any other woman I would want to marry.'

'Well, then I will . . .'

The door opened and Catherine swept into the room. 'And what are you two in conclave about?' she asked buoyantly.

'Just cricket,' Morton said airily.

'I did not think you were very interested in cricket, Papa!'

'I am interested in anything that keeps these colonials in their places,' her father said smugly.

Catherine gave him a puzzled glance, then turned to Morton. 'Come along, James,' she said. 'We must hurry, if we are to catch our train. I have telegraphed my aunt; so they will stay luncheon for us.'

An empty growler was trotting down Park Lane, and Morton waved it down. The streets were comparatively empty, and they had some minutes to spare before the train was due to depart. He settled down opposite Catherine, feeling the stirrings of a new kind of happiness. Was it that he appeared to have received her father's blessing? Surely not; for she would do as she pleased, regardless of his views. No, it was that they would be together for the rest of the day; that she was happy and animated; that with her he could forget the tension and gloom at the Priory . . . Perhaps also, that they both might glimpse what life could be like.

'You are pensive, James,' Catherine said teasingly.

'I was thinking about my conversation with your father.'

95

'About cricket?'

He laughed. 'No, before that. About the paintings in the Cornhill Gallery.'

Her smile faded. 'Oh? Was he helpful?' she asked.

'Extremely so. I shall be able to tell Sergeant Bragg, with complete confidence, that they are not what they seem.'

'They are forgeries?'

'According to your esteemed father.'

'I see ... So, the late Clifford Needham did not have to be wealthy, if his Constable came from the same source.'

'Good heavens! I had not thought about that. You are a good many jumps ahead of us.'

'Why? Sergeant Bragg postulates a link between Needham's murder and the Cornhill Gallery. Needham has a painting he could not possibly afford. Wicks's gallery contains old masters that are forgeries. I would have thought it was obvious!'

Morton gave a rueful smile. 'I very much fear,' he said, 'that your relentless logic has just demolished all our theories about the case!'

Four hours later, they were sitting in the Knightons' carriage, on the way to Chilcomb. The road was rough; the noise made conversation difficult. So they sat opposite each other, looking at the fresh greens of the countryside. Catherine mentally shook herself. Winchester always had this effect on her. Her roots were here, rather than London; emotionally anyway. The Knightons' house had been her mother's family home. Her parents had lived there briefly, after they married. Under its roof, her own life had been conceived. She had always felt safe and cosseted there. In a special way, it had been home to her ... But not today. Aunt Phoebe had fussed around James, intent on anticipating his every wish. At first, Catherine had been flattered. It was mildly satisfying to have James treated as if he were virtually one of the family. Particularly as she retained the power to spurn him, if she chose. But cousin Elizabeth had not regarded James as spoken for. She had openly flirted with him; positively sparkled. Well she might! At twenty-two, and with the restricted possibilities in a country town like Winchester, her chances of making a good marriage must be diminishing month by month. Yet Catherine had to acknowledge a moment of panic. Men were stupid. Their heads could be turned by a flutter of eyelashes. All a girl had to do was look helpless and vulnerable, and they would come running. Well, she would not pretend to be a helpless ninny for any man!

She roused herself, as the carriage turned into the drive of Chilcomb House. It was a substantial mansion, on the edge of the village.

'You will have to forsake your reverie,' Morton said with a smile.

'I will sit in the carriage,' Catherine said petulantly. 'It hardly seems worthwhile coming in with you.'

'But you might think of something I had missed,' Morton said. 'Please come too.'

Catherine allowed herself to be persuaded. Soon they were waiting in a sunlit drawing-room, while a servant sought the master of the house. Eventually a stocky grey-haired man came in. He looked surprised.

'Mary told me it was the police,' he said.

Morton produced his warrant-card. 'I have certainly come on a police matter,' he said. 'In the course of an investigation, in London, we discovered a long-case clock that we believe to be your property.'

'Have you, by God!' Fulton exclaimed.

'We checked with William Smith's factory. It was they who gave us your address. I wanted to find out if you had sold the clock.'

'Sold it? Indeed I did not!' Fulton said emphatically. 'It was stolen from this house, together with many other items of value.'

'When was this?' Morton asked.

'Last Christmas. We were away as a family. Only some of the servants remained here. The thieves must have had informants in the village. We have never been given to flaunting our wealth; only good families visit us. Of course, plenty of the locals would know we were away. That's the worst of it; wondering who betrayed us.'

'I take it that your property was covered by insurance,' Morton said.

'Yes, indeed The City of London Fire. Good company. They paid up without a murmur.'

'I see. As you will have gathered, sir, we hope to return your clock to you, in due course. And we might well find some of the other items stolen from you.'

Fulton frowned. 'I would hardly want to go along with that,' he said. 'We have spent the claim money on replacements. Had to! I could not repay that amount to the insurance company; I am not flush with the stuff. Anyway, we have got used to being without them, now.'

'I see, sir,' Morton said. 'Could you at least let us have a list of the items you lost?'

'No, I could not!' Fulton said angrily. 'Get it from the insurance people!'

7

On Monday morning, Bragg was already waiting in Sir Rufus Stone's chambers, when the coroner came in. He avoided Bragg's eye and marched into his room. Bragg had to wait, in growing impatience, for almost half an hour before the clerk approached him.

'Sir Rufus will see you now,' he murmured.

When Bragg entered, Sir Rufus waved him to a chair and continued his perusal of a voluminous brief. Finally he pushed it aside. 'Well, Bragg?' he asked coldly.

'I have come for instructions, sir. Inspector Cotton has delegated the Needham case back to me.'

'Hah! So my strategy has been successful!' the coroner exclaimed. 'I drew them into a false position, and they have capitulated. Excellent!'

'Yes, sir,' Bragg said drily.

'Well, Bragg, what instructions do you want? You have to identify and arrest the murderer of Needham! There can be no other course.'

'I have more or less been told to write the case off as a footpadding.'

The coroner's eyes narrowed. 'But you do not agree with that expedient.'

'No, sir. You see, Needham's father, though he came from a professional background, was by no stretch of the imagination wealthy.'

'What profession, Bragg?'

'He was a solicitor, sir.'

'I can well believe it, Bragg! The law is a vastly under-rewarded profession. A man will lay out his treasure unstintingly, to be hacked about by some butcher in a white coat. But, ask him to pay a comparatively modest amount to be guided through the intricacies of the law, and he is resentful.'

'Yes, sir.'

'However, you are deviating from the purpose of your visit. We have established that Needham's family was not rich. What flows from that?'

'He, himself, was in salaried employment; always had been,' Bragg said. 'Yet I find that large sums of cash were being paid into the bank account he had at Windsor.'

'Hmm . . . Are you suggesting corruption? There are some distasteful stories circulating concerning Needham, but nothing touching on his business integrity. In any case, what could he possibly provide in exchange? . . . Mind you, with income tax at the present ruinous level of six pence in the pound, one can only expect nefarious attempts to avoid it . . . Not condone, you understand, but expect, certainly.'

'We have no actual evidence of misconduct, sir. And these credits go right back to the time he lived in Windsor . . . But there is one odd thing. Of late, these cash deposits have come from the National Provincial branch in Lothbury.'

'In the City! Has he an account at that branch?'

'I have not had time to check, sir.'

The coroner glared at him. 'Then, I suggest that you do so . . . Lothbury, eh? Does that imply a City source for the cash?'

'It might do.'

'Perhaps he was advising people, independently of his employment?'

Bragg pondered. 'I cannot see there is much scope for that,' he said at length. 'Anyway, it would be frowned on by his employers.'

'Undoubtedly. But when has that been an absolute bar to such activities?'

'Of course,' Bragg said, 'it might have had nothing to do with his employment.'

Sir Rufus glared at him. 'I have been a barrister for far too long, to enjoy being led by the nose in this way, Bragg. If you have a hypothesis, please propound it!'

'Very well, sir. As you know, Needham was found in Change Alley.'

'Inside an undertaker's van, yes.'

'I believe Needham was murdered there and, in the struggle, a window was broken in some adjoining premises – the Cornhill Gallery.'

'So?'

'Wicks, the proprietor of the gallery, lied to us.'

'I hope, Bragg, that you have not resolved on a course of hanging every man who embroiders the truth,' Sir Rufus said sardonically.

'No, sir. It was more deliberate than that. According to our beat constable – and he is a Salvationist – the window was intact at eleven, and broken at twelve on the Sunday; that is the night of the murder. Now, Wicks told me that the window had been broken on the Saturday night, by some boys larking about. He swears he saw it all happen from his apartment, over the shop.'

'I see. But, surely, had he been personally involved in a criminal enterprise, during which the window was broken, his first instinct would have been to have the shattered glass replaced.'

'I was on the scene by ten o'clock on the Monday morning.'

The coroner mused. 'I have but little acquaintance with these things,' he said at length. 'But I would have thought it likely that, in an emergency, it would be perfectly possible to have a window reglazed at any time from six o'clock on a weekday morning. It is strange that, as you say, he prevaricated over the matter. But, by itself, it is nothing.'

Bragg hesitated. 'Well, there is something else,' he said. 'We have reason to suppose that the gallery itself may be connected to criminal activities.'

'Hah! How is that?'

'That block of buildings is leased by a company called George Barber Ltd. That selfsame company holds the lease of a small warehouse at eight, Crooked Lane.'

'So?'

'We happened to be in the store recently, sir, and Constable Morton took down the maker's number from the dial of a clock. We have since discovered that the clock had been stolen.'

'You seem to be clutching at straws, Bragg!' Sir Rufus said contemptuously. 'You appear to be assuming that this company leased both premises to the same person, which may be totally unwarranted. Further it is perfectly possible that the clock you refer to has passed through several pairs of hands since it was stolen. I am prepared to accept that its only legitimate owner is the person from whom it was stolen. But I am not thereby prepared to proclaim its present possessor a criminal! Now, if that is the meagre extent of your information, be off with you! I have a living to earn.'

'Well, sir,' Bragg said slowly, 'over the weekend we did follow up on the clock. Constable Morton and a young lady went to see the man it was made for. It appears it was stolen when the family was away, at Christmas.'

'So recently?'

'Yes. Now, this young lady was in the Cornhill Gallery recently. She explained that she was about to be married; so she was able to have a good look round. One of the things Wicks said to her was that, if there was anything she particularly wanted, he would do his level best to get it for her.'

'And very laudable, too. I do not see where this is leading.'

'But, suppose he had a way of locating what she wanted; of having it stolen from its rightful owners, to sell to her.'

'Well? Get to the point, man!'

'As I see it, sir, the very person who could give him that kind of information was Clifford Needham. When someone of substance insures his property, he has to give a detailed schedule of what is to be covered by the insurance. Needham, as general manager, was in the position of being able to open any file; take it away to look at it, if he chose. Suppose somebody said to him: "Who has got a Broadwood grand piano?" I bet he could have had five names and addresses in an hour.'

'An interesting supposition, Bragg. Can you put flesh on it?'

'Well, the man who had the clock stolen was insured with Needham's company.'

Sir Rufus's eyes narrowed. 'I see . . . But what we do not have is evidence of a connection between Needham and Wicks.'

'Only the painting, sir.'

'I would have you know,' the coroner said irritably, 'that I find this oblique method of exposition nearer to obfuscation than elucidation. Have the goodness to tell me plainly what you know!'

'Very good, sir. In Wicks's shop there are lots of paintings, each with its little card tucked in the corner of its frame, saying "Constable", "Reynolds", "Gainsborough".'

Sir Rufus raised his eyebrows. 'I did not realise that it was an establishment of such quality,' he said.

'And you would be right, sir. I had the paintings looked at, on the quiet, by an expert. Some of them, anyway. He reckons they are forgeries.'

'You mean fakes?'

'Yes, sir.'

'The name of this expert?' Sir Rufus asked suspiciously.

'William Marsden RA.'

'I see. A fellow painter, rather than an art historian.'

'Yes, sir. He says that, although you might think they were genuine at first sight, the forger has not been able to imitate the technique of Gainsborough and Constable.'

'Very well, where does this get us?'

'Well, it suggests to me that Wicks is setting out to defraud the public, for a start. If so, it supports my theory that he could be in a kind of burglary-to-order plot with Needham.'

'Huh! You will have to do better than that, Bragg!' Sir Rufus said contemptuously. 'It would appear that I must repeat myself; you have not yet demonstrated that the two men even knew each other.'

'Well, sir, the Needhams have a Constable painting on their sitting-room wall, that is very like the one in Wicks's shop.'

'And where does that take us?'

'It could have come from Wicks; show that they knew each other.'

Sir Rufus stared out of the window for a space, then turned to Bragg. 'I cannot accept that it will suffice,' he said. 'The unsupported view of a practising painter would hardly be enough to convince a jury that these paintings were fakes. Until that is achieved, Wicks must be regarded as an honest man. As to the burglary-to-order theory; even on your presuppositions, a jury would need much more evidence before it could properly be directed to convict. No, Bragg, at the moment your theories are ingenious, but scarcely even plausible.'

Morton went into the Cornhill Gallery, in the hope Bronwen would be there, but he looked around in vain. He cleared his throat noisily. At that, a man appeared from the back of the shop. Presumably it was Wicks.

'Can I be of assistance?' he asked, in a warm ingratiating voice.

'I am just browsing,' Morton said amiably. 'But, could you tell me the name of the person who wove that tapestry? It is rather fine.'

Wicks almost purred. 'It is a particularly fine example of a Bronwen Price,' he said. 'She is a quite outstanding artist. Her work is very difficult to get hold of!'

Morton frowned. 'But it is rather large,' he said doubtfully. 'I hardly know where I could hang it.'

Wicks gave a tolerant smile, and turned towards a woman who had just entered, her arms full of parcels. He took up a strategic position, to protect a display of fine china and glass. Then he became involved in an argument with her, about a piece of furniture which had been scratched, in transit from the shop to her home.

Morton went over to the back wall. The Stubbs had not yet been sold. He looked at the detail critically. The carriage... It was a two-wheeled gig, the seat made like a spindle-backed chair. And, surely the body was mounted on platform springs? One could just see the end of the spring on which the body was bolted. Without doubt, it was a Stanhope gig. Hardly surprising in itself. That design had become extremely popular, as a light carriage for two people. So, why should that cause him unease? But the painting had troubled Sergeant Bragg also. And that was more significant, because he was a carter's son; had spent his youth among vehicles of every kind. Morton tried to remember who had built the Stanhope gig. Its specifications had been determined by the Hon. Fitzroy Stanhope, that he did know. But who had built it? Not Lawtons, or Bennett... Of course! With that design of seat, it must have been made by Tilbury! Well, he could easily set his mind at rest. He went out of the shop, and waved down a passing hansom.

In twenty minutes, he was in the office of Tilbury's works in Islington. The clerk peered at his warrant-card, and his face lit up. 'You must be Jim Morton, the cricketer!' he exclaimed. 'Fine job you did in Australia!' He held out his hand. 'It's an honour to meet you, sir.'

'Thank you,' Morton said in embarrassment. 'Now, I wonder if you can give me some information.'

'Certainly!'

'When did you begin to build the Stanhope gig?'

'Cor! That's a tall order,' the clerk said. 'It must be ages ago. We were just about building the last of them, when I came here, twenty-five years ago. Lawton's Liverpool gig took over; and we concentrated on heavier vehicles.'

'Surely you must have records?'

'Well, yes. But not here; not that far back.'

'It is extremely important,' Morton said earnestly.

'A case, is it?'

'Yes, indeed. A murder case.'

'Cor! I'll tell you what, why don't we go into the workshop? Bill Johnson, the foreman, might know. He's been here even longer than me!'

Morton followed the clerk across the yard, to a long low building. He could hear the noise of hammering and sawing. Outside, a new landau gleamed in the sun, still smelling of varnish. Inside the workshop, were vehicles in various stages of completion.

'This is Mr Johnson,' the clerk said, then turned to the foreman. 'And this is Jim Morton, the cricketer. He wants a word.'

Morton held out his hand. 'I am glad to see that you are still building phaetons,' he said. 'My father has one of your spider phaetons; it is a splendid drive!'

'A rich man's toy,' Johnson said, without rancour.

'Mr Morton is a policeman,' the clerk interposed. 'He has something to ask you.'

'Yes, indeed!' Morton said. 'And I am afraid that I am going to ask you to delve even further into the past.'

'Oh, yes?'

'Can you tell me when the first Stanhope gig was made?'

Johnson scratched his head. 'Not offhand, I can't. Before I came, that's for sure.' He frowned, then his face cleared. 'I know,' he said. 'It's got to be on the drawings!'

He led the way into a small office, in the far corner of the workshop. Along one wall was a range of cupboards. The centre of the floor was taken up by a large square table. Johnson referred briefly to a small ledger, then went over to a cupboard. He peered along the shelves, then came back triumphantly with a working drawing and laid it on the table. It was headed: 'A two-wheeled gig, for the Hon. Fitzroy Stanhope'. Johnson pointed to a date at the bottom. It was the fourth of May, 1815.

Catherine was walking along Aldgate High Street, after lunch. She wanted to be sure of her ground, before putting her proposals to the editor, Mr Tranter. The City of London was often accused of being inward-looking, self-absorbed. There was truth in it, of course. Compared to the areas to the east and north, the City was immeasurably wealthy. But the detractors were not telling the whole truth. There were many charitable foundations in the poor areas around, which had been set up, and were still maintained, with charitable funds from the City. The Jews Free School was a case in point . . . Indeed, Spitalfields would merit an article in its own right. She could describe the flight of the Huguenot silk-weavers from France, to sanctuary in the area. She might even persuade Mr Tranter to print an etching of some of their houses, or the Hawksmoor church. Then, for people not of a historical bent, there was the splendid modern market-hall. After Spital-fields she could do an article on Whitechapel; then Bethnal Green, another old silkweaving area . . . A movement distracted her . . . Someone cutting in ahead of her from a side-street. A man strolling along, an outline that was familiar . . . She quickened her pace. It was James! What on earth was he doing, so far into the area of the Metropolitan police? Of course, he could be investigating a crime that had been committed in the City. But his demeanour hardly suggested that. She set herself to follow him, her curiosity spiced with excitement. She had been involved with him in many cases; but not to the point where he arrested a suspect. It would be a new experience for her. He turned left into Goulston Street . . . But his demeanour was hardly that of a policeman on the point of capturing someone . . . If she had to put a word to it, his walk was jaunty. He turned left into New Goulston Street. She broke into a run to get to the corner before she lost him. Yes, there he was, strolling along. She felt a flash of shame to be following him – spying on him. But there was no harm in it. Sometime she would tell him of it; they would laugh together, feel close and happy ... Now he was turning into Love Court. So far as she could remember, it was a cul-de-sac. So this was not a mere lunch-time stroll; he must be going to see someone. In that case, she must not become involved. She ought to keep well away, she told herself. Love Court ... The very name filled her with foreboding. She reached the corner and peered round. James had stopped in front of a house, was knocking on the door. He stepped back and looked upwards. After a moment, one of the upper windows was pushed up. A woman's head appeared; a young woman. Catherine could hear her laugh; a bang as the window was shut ... Then the front door was opened; the woman came gaily into the street, there was an exchange of words, laughter. She laid her hand on his arm and drew him inside.

Bronwen took Morton up to her father's studio, and introduced them. Evan Price was of medium height and powerful build. He looked to be in his mid-forties. Bushy eyebrows jutted over eyes as violet-blue as his daughter's; flecks of grey speckled his untidy brown hair. His shirt-sleeves were rolled up his muscular, hairy arms. He wiped his hand on a piece of rag tucked into the waistband of his trousers and shook hands.

'I am very pleased to meet you, Mr Morton,' he said with a smile. The Welsh lilt in his voice was more pronounced than was Bronwen's. The nude had disappeared from his easel. In its place was an old painting on its stretcher. Most of it was covered in brown varnish, so thick that the scene beneath it was virtually obscured. The bottom left-hand corner, however, was fresh and bright. Morton could see green grass, the yellow flecks of tiny flowers. Price dabbed at the brown varnish with a pad of cloth.

'I am expected to find a Kneller under all this filth,' he said. 'But I fear the owner will be disappointed ... I may have to whistle for my fee.'

'Surely not?' Morton said. 'The restorer can hardly be blamed for an erroneous attribution.'

'You would be surprised, young man. Extreme disappointment can have a very odd effect on a man's ethical standards. No matter that the effort of restoring is the same, whether the picture is an old master, or a pot-boiler by an unknown; if the owner's hopes are dashed, he will begrudge paying you.'

'Why, then, do you do it?'

Price shrugged. 'Not for the money, I can tell you . . . I suppose every job is a voyage of discovery. It might be an unknown old master. You could find yourself giving a Holbein back to the world, that has hung in some fusty corner of an old house . . . It's the excitement, you see.' He beckoned to Morton. 'Look at that spot of white appearing against the grass. What will it be? A lady's kerchief, a fallen flower, a child's ribbon . . . Much better than churning out prettified pictures for Philistines!'

Morton felt Bronwen's hand caressing his thigh, pulling him down to sit by her on the sofa.

'You originally came from South Wales, your daughter tells me,' Morton said, capturing her hand.

'Cardiff. Would that I could have stayed there! But fate decreed otherwise.'

'Fate?' Morton asked.

'Must have been! I'd always been handy with pencil and brush. My teacher would have me try for a scholarship at the Slade School of Art . . . I think it might be a rose, a white rose . . . Well, coming from the Celtic fringes, I didn't get the scholarship. But they did award me an exhibition. Which kept me just above the level of starvation for three years. I came out with a diploma, and no chance of earning my living. I hawked my pictures round the dealers for three months, then decided to go back to Wales.'

'That was when you met Mam,' Bronwen chipped in.

'That's right. I was working on Cardiff docks, when I met her. Humping coal on to ships, that sailed round the coast to Bristol and London. Back-breaking, mindless work it was. But I stuck at it, got married, begat a daughter.' He smiled proudly at Bronwen, then turned back to his work. 'We lived with the wife's sister,' he went on. 'Monmouth Road . . . Yes, it is some sort of flower. Maybe the woman in the picture has dropped a camelia – or thrown it away . . . Then my luck changed. I met a shipowner, with money to burn. He had built a medieval castle at Rudry, between Cardiff and Newport. Funny idea, isn't it. I expect he wanted everybody to think that his ancestors had come over with William the Conqueror. But everybody knew his grandfather had humped bags of coal round Cardiff . . . Anyway, he wanted me to decorate this castle with frescoes, in the Italian manner. I jumped at the chance. My wife was a cultured, middle-class girl. Too good for me, by half. She looked up Welsh legends in the library, and I would paint them round the windows and across the walls of the baronial hall. Owen Glendower chasing the English out of Wales! Not something I could be proud of, but it kept us in comfort. Fancy us, living in a castle! . . . Then came the cholera, and my wife died. My in-laws took Bronwen in, and I ran away to London again.' He stepped back. 'I think I shall leave the central figure till tomorow,' he said. 'If you are not fresh, you can easily do more harm than good.'

'So, what happened when you came back to London?' Morton asked.

Bronwen squeezed his arm. 'Auntie wouldn't let me go, until Dad could show them he could take care of me,' she said.

Price smiled indulgently. 'Yes, they were dark days. I worked as a house-painter for three years; doing occasional portraits of people not much better off than myself. Then I bumped into Gideon Wicks. I had known him at the Slade. He had been more interested in the history of art, so it was no surprise to find him running an art gallery. Not the one he has now; one out in Kensington. Anyway, he asked me to restore some old paintings, and I found I had a flair for it. More to the point, I enjoyed it.'

Morton turned to Bronwen. 'And where did you learn to weave?' he asked.

'In Cardiff, of course! Where else?'

Price cleaned his hands with spirit, then went over to the corner and picked up a picture. He brought it over to Morton.

'I had a canvas with the ground already on it, so I was able to begin your brother's portrait.'

Morton gazed at it. 'That is remarkable!' he said.

'Of course, it will have to dry for a few more days, before I can finish it.'

'But you have done wonders! I could really believe that he would have looked precisely like that. It is quite amazing!'

Price gave a satisfied grunt. 'It was a challenge,' he said. 'I've never been asked to do this before.'

'I am most indebted to you!' Morton said warmly. 'You must let me pay you your fee on account.'

Price smiled at his daughter. 'I understand,' he said, 'that Bronwen has that in hand . . . Now, I am just going out for an hour.'

8

'Some times I do not know which side Sir Rufus is on!' Bragg said next morning, poking disconsolately in the bowl of his pipe. 'I had over an hour with him, yesterday. He seemed to relish knocking over every idea I put up. Refused to countenance any connection between Wicks's shop, and the warehouse where we found the stolen clock. He is even holding back from that; saying it could have passed through several hands, in the last four months.'

'That seems uncharacteristically cautious,' Morton said lightly.

'Huh! I reckon he got into hot water, over the naming of Denison and Hunter as suspects, in his court,' Bragg said darkly. 'There was no need for him to call Inspector Cotton. It must have seemed to some people, that he wanted it to come out.'

'So, his mighty brain could contribute nothing?'

'Unless telling me that we haven't been able to show any connection between Wicks and Needham is a contribution.'

'Miss Marsden pointed out another unwelcome aspect of our case, on Sunday.' Morton said, with a rueful smile. 'If the Constable painting in Needham's house is not genuine, but supplied by his supposed friend, Wicks, there is no need to postulate the illicit wealth to pay for it.'

'Huh! The whole blasted case seems to be coming to bits in our hands ... And yet Needham was a villain; I am convinced of it. Forget the painting; there is still a load of cash we cannot account for. You remember the amounts marked "N.P.Lothbury", in the Windsor account?'

'Yes.'

'I went along there, yesterday.'

'To the National Provincial in Lothbury?'

'Yes. At first, I expected them to unearth an account in Needham's name. But he had no such thing I gave them the dates of the credits in the Windsor account; said the manager there had told me they came from Lothbury ... In the end they tracked them down. Needham must have gone to the counter, with a great wad of banknotes, and asked for them to be credited to his account with their Windsor branch.'

'Why such a convoluted procedure?' Morton asked.

'Because he was up to no good, that's why. Because it was money he could not account for honestly!'

'But, even accepting that ...'

There was a tap at the door, and the Commissioner wandered in. He peered out of the window for some moments, then turned.

'I sometimes think, Bragg,' he said plaintively, 'that I am no more than a fairground coconut shy, for any Tom, Dick and Harry to throw stones at. I have just endured a most acrimonious halfhour with some members of the Watch Committee. They say there are rumours of a crazed killer, stalking the City streets. Their employees are petitioning to be allowed to leave their offices early, so as to be home in daylight.'

'But that is stupid!' Bragg said. 'It is light until well after seven now. They are imagining things!'

'They are not imagining the murders of two insurance men – from the same company, moreover.'

'There has not been a killing for over a week now, sir.'

'And, when was the first?' Sir William asked irritably.

'Three weeks before Needham, sir.'

'Well, then! Hardly a sound position to defend. I am under pressure to put more men on the beat, to reassure the public. But, where do I get them from? We are under-manned, as it is. Do I go to the Metropolitan Police Commissioner on my bended knees? Ask him to lend me some of his officers to patrol the City's streets? It would be just the opening he is waiting for, Bragg. Our existence is an anomaly, he would say. An administrative absurdity, to have a square mile in the middle of his area, policed by an independent force. And, make no mistake, the Home Office would back him up!'

'The City fathers would never stand for it, sir,' Bragg said encouragingly. 'At bottom, they know that they have the best-trained, best-led police force in the world.'

'Do you think so, Bragg?' Sir William asked gratefully.

'Indeed I do, sir. And as for the investigation, that is down to the coroner.'

The Commissioner sighed. 'I know that is the theory – perhaps more than a theory, in the City, unfortunately. But the aldermen pay me to preserve their peace, not the coroner. It is to me that they come for results.'

'Yes. Well, the second case did not get off to the best of starts,' Bragg said blandly. 'Anyway, to Inspector Cotton's way of thinking, Needham was killed by a bludger for his money, not a maniac.'

'Yes ... I urged that on the aldermen, but they would have none of it. And I had to admit that the notecase of Purvis, the clerk, was not taken.'

Bragg smoothed his ragged moustache. 'Then again, if the inspector is right, why was Needham put into the undertaker's van?'

'You mean that it is not the action of a sane person?' the Commisioner asked unhappily.

'Hardly, is it?'

'You bring me little comfort, Bragg. I suppose my only course is to exhort the men on the beat to increase their vigilance.' Sir William sighed, and wandered out again.

'Poor old sod!' Bragg said feelingly. 'Why didn't he stick to soldiering, where everything is done by numbers? What time is it, lad?'

'A quarter to ten.'

'Where was it Miss Marsden's article said Needham went to school?'

'Malmesbury, in Wiltshire.'

'Get down the Bradshaw, lad. See what time we can catch a train to Malmesbury.'

Morton turned the pages slowly. 'Malmesbury does not appear to be on a railway line, sir,' he said. 'It seems one should travel to Swindon.'

'And, how far after that?'

Morton shrugged. 'Fifteen or eighteen miles, I suppose.'

'Blast it! That will be all day of a job. When is the next train?'

'Twenty-past eleven, from Paddington.'

'Right. Let us bestir ourselves.'

*

Despite his earlier irritation, Bragg found himself enjoying the journey. Once out of London and its suburbs, the train passed through a patchwork of countryside and small towns. They stopped for a time at Slough, so that passengers for Windsor could alight. Was it still less than a week since he had changed at this station, to go to Needham's funeral? But the thought was of no comfort to him. How much progress had they made in that time? Inspector Cotton would answer it in one word. None! And the coroner seemed to agree with him. Yet, whatever the inspector thought, Sir Rufus believed there was more to it than a casual footpadding. At least he was on Bragg's side. But he wanted results, too. Bragg tried to concentrate his mind, to fight off the drowsiness induced by the gentle motion of the train, the clickety-clack as it sped over the rails. There had to be a pattern . . . Even if Needham's picture was a fake, there must be a link . . . Because Needham's picture . . .

He woke with Morton shaking his arm.

'This is Swindon, sir,' he was saying. 'We get off here.'

They found a smart trap, with a sprightly-looking horse, in the station yard. On learning that the driver wanted three shillings to drive them to Malmesbury and back, Bragg waxed indignant. By dint of pressing the coins into the driver's hand, Morton ended the altercation, and they set off. It was fortunate, he thought, that it was a fine day. Even beyond the limits of Swindon town, the road surfaces were good. And it was the kind of day that lifted the spirits; sent the blood coursing through one's veins. The hedgerows were bright green in the sunlight; the lush grass at their foot was sprinkled with yellow flowers. It was a countryside idyll – there was even a farm labourer with his dog, eating his lunch under an oak tree. It was the countryside as middle-class sentimentalists believed it to be. Placid, verdant, Arcadian. Far from the reality of back-breaking, unremitting toil; whose fruits might well be spoiled by fickle weather . . . A woolly cloud drifted over the sun. As the scene darkened, so did Morton's mood. He had to admit that, as a youth, he had envied his brother; resented the assumption that Edwin would succeed to the family estates. That had been displaced by a feeling of guilt, when Edwin had been brought home from the Sudan grievously wounded. Yet the guilt had been tempered by moments of elation; for surely Edwin would never be able to run the estates now? But he had underestimated the depths of his parents' compassion. By then, Sir Henry had retired from the army. He had been appointed to the largely honorific post of Lord-Lieutenant of Kent. And he was obviously enjoying the experience of running the estates – which had belonged to his family since the dissolution of the monasteries.

Yet, when Edwin's wound had begun to heal, Sir Henry had pronounced that, henceforward, Edwin should manage the estates. It was patently absurd. He was paralysed from the waist down. The slightest cough or infection, and they feared for his life. The upshot of it all was that no one ran them. His father steadfastly refused to acknowledge that the farms were going to rack and ruin. Edwin, on a balmy summer's day, might be carried down to the dogcart, or the Daimler automobile, and be driven round the lanes. But, for the most part, he lay propped up in bed, with charts of the fields and crops. The bailiff would go to see him each morning, receive his instructions, then go and do what he thought best.

It was that situation which had made Morton leave the Priory. In a quixotic moment, he had taken up a casual remark at a dinner party. The guests had been discussing modern youth; their lack of adventurous spirit, now that the empire had been won and settled. He had made an intemperate comment. What it was, he had long forgotten. But the Commissioner of the City of London police had been at the table. He had challenged Morton to join his force; to begin at the bottom, and experience the real world. Nor had Morton ever regretted taking up the gauntlet. Sir William Sumner had readily agreed that he could take leave of absence to play cricket. But he had stipulated that this was to be the only concession. That apart, he would be treated as any other recruit; would compete for promotion on equal terms with them.

He had served now for six enjoyable years; most of them under Sergeant Bragg. He had received no favours; had experienced the pleasure of doing a difficult job to the satisfaction of his superiors. Yet he had to admit that, at the back of his mind, there was always the assumption that he would go back to Ashwell Priory; in time, take over the running of the estates. A single Dervish bullet had ordained that. Now, rattling through the countryside, he wondered if it was really what he wanted. Edwin's death might not trigger an acceptance in his parents that he ought to take over.

Certainly, his father would be capable of running the estates for years yet . . . But that was hardly the point. Once he was the only heir, their expectations, as yet unvoiced, must descend on his shoulders. It was that, of course, which had irked him all these years. Their implacable refusal to accept that the estates must pass to him, or through him. Were he to marry, produce an heir, they would be compelled to acknowledge reality . . . If only Catherine were not so wedded to her career, so consumed with ambition . . .

The driver turned round. 'See that church spire?' he asked. 'That's Malmesbury.'

Bragg bestirred himself. 'Take us to St Jude's school,' he said. 'And wait for us.'

Twenty minutes later they were bowling down a gravelled drive, to a cluster of red-brick buildings.

'Funny sort of place,' Bragg said. 'I can't see a child anywhere.'

'It will be the Easter holidays,' Morton said. 'There seems to be a house behind the chapel. My guess is that the headmaster will live there.'

They left the trap, and walked over to the house. As they approached it, they saw a shirt-sleeved man bending over some rose bushes by the front door. He straightened up. He had a round, pink face and balding head. He was wearing a clerical collar and stock.

'We are looking for the headmaster,' Bragg called.

'I am he!' The man dropped his pruning knife on the path, and came to meet them.

'We are officers of the City of London police,' Bragg said, proffering his warrant-card.

'Goodness me! I view the visit of any police officer with trepidation,' the headmaster said. 'But for someone to come so far . . .'

'Don't worry, sir,' Bragg said amiably. 'It's not one of your current crop we are concerned about. I don't suppose you are aware of the murder of a man called Needham – Clifford Needham?'

'No.'

'It happened in London, where he lives. We know he was educated at this school.'

'I see. I am afraid that I have been headmaster for only ten years. I do not recall the name.'

'He was in his mid-forties,' Bragg said. 'That would suggest he must have been a pupil here in the early 1860s.'

'I presume we will have records for that period,' the headmaster said reluctantly. 'But I fail to see how they could possibly help you.'

'We are clutching at straws, sir, I'll grant you that,' Bragg said confidingly. 'But it is our clear duty.'

'Yes . . . Well, there are some old register-books, and so on, in a press in the office. I suppose we might examine them.'

He led the way to one of the classroom blocks, along a corridor, to an office overlooking a quadrangle. He unlocked a wooden cupboard and revealed shelf upon shelf of record-books and files.

'Shall we try 1865?' he suggested.

He carried a ledger to a table under the window, and began to turn the pages. 'Ah, here we are! Clifford Needham. Yes, he was a senior boy by then . . . We should have a file on one of these shelves.' He went back to the cupboard and, squatting down, began to go through bundles of papers. Then he grunted with satisfaction, and stood up.

'Here we are,' he said. He glanced through the papers and a wary look crossed his face. 'What is it you wish to know?' he asked.

'Well . . . anything you have got, sir. You can never tell what bit of seemingly useless information will strike a chord.'

'I see,' the headmaster said reluctantly. 'Well, Clifford Needham came to this school, at the usual age of nine, in 1859.'

'Which would make him forty-five or six now. That seems to be right, doesn't it, constable?'

'Yes, sir.'

'What can you tell us about him?' Bragg asked.

'Why . . . he seems initially to have been rather reserved; but that is by no means unusual in a young boy.'

'Was he a clever lad?'

The headmaster scanned a sheet of paper from the file. 'Yes, reasonably so,' he said. 'He was perhaps not as industrious as one would have liked. I see that several of his teachers thought that he was not fulfilling his potential, but . . .' His voice faded; he put the sheet back in the file and closed it.

'The school was disappointed in him, then?' Bragg persisted.

116

'Not scholastically, sergeant. Indeed my predecessor was able to recommend him warmly, to the Imperial Fire Insurance Company, when they asked for a reference.'

'If not scholastically, then what?'

The headmaster looked out of the window. 'One sometimes encounters problems, in a community of growing boys,' he said reluctantly. 'Not all relationships are of a wholly desirable nature ... And I fear Needham was a case in point. He seems to have formed an attachment to an older boy. It would appear that the usual admonition did not suffice, for he was subsequently transferred from School House to Latimer House.'

'That did the trick, did it, sir?' Bragg asked sardonically.

The headmaster looked at him coldly. 'So far as appears from the records,' he said.

'I see ... And would the name of this older boy be Gideon Wicks, by any chance?'

A look of surprise spread over the headmaster's face. 'Why, yes,' he said. 'Indeed it was.'

Bragg and Morton did not converse as the trap took them back to Swindon station. And they arrived just as the London train was pulling into the platform. The compartment was fairly full already, so there was no opportunity for conversation. Indeed, the train had reached Maidenhead before they were left alone. Then Bragg knocked out his pipe in the ashtray.

'So, what do you think now, lad?' he asked.

'About Needham, you mean?'

'Who else?'

Morton smiled. 'Having been educated at home, by tutors, I can hardly comment.'

'Huh! I sometimes wonder how you turned out so normal ... But, from the sound of it, Needham would have done well in the navy! Anyway, the important thing is that connections are appearing. Needham and Wicks at school together, Wicks and Price at the Slade together. Even by the coroner's standards, that puts Wicks in the middle of the picture.'

'But what evidence have we that Wicks was connected with the murder of Needham – to say nothing of the clerk Purvis?'

'We don't know they were connected,' Bragg said placidly.

'But you believe that they were.'

'As you go through life, you will realise that coincidences can be fruitful.'

'In an evidential sense?'

'What else?'

Morton considered briefly. 'Is it not straining credulity to think that Wicks and Needham would have kept up a friendship over all these years?'

'I don't think so, lad. It was a special sort of friendship. Don't forget, there is no mention of a Mrs Wicks, past or present.'

'So, where does that leave us?'

'Well, it's my belief that Wicks gave that so-called Constable to Mrs Needham. If it came from the same source as the one in the gallery now, it wouldn't have cost him a lot. And it would have got him into her good books.'

'I suppose so.'

'And we can bring Wicks's other connection in too. I reckon Price painted it.'

Morton frowned. 'There is not the remotest evidence to support that theory,' he said irritably. 'I have been to his studio.'

'When was this?' Bragg demanded.

'Yesterday morning. Bronwen invited me there. She has asked her father to paint a portrait, from a photograph of my brother Edwin. When I was there, he was in the process of cleaning the varnish from a painting supposedly by Sir Godfrey Kneller.'

'"Bronwen invited me there,"' Bragg mimicked him savagely. 'What the hell are you doing? Price is a bloody suspect! If you were a soldier, they would shoot you for consorting with the enemy!'

'We have found no evidence whatever to support that,' Morton said angrily. 'And I am not prepared to live my life on the off-chance that an acquaintance may turn out to have committed a crime! I happen to admire Miss Price very much. She has had a difficult childhood; yet she is a warm and charming young lady. I believe that she is a considerable artist in her own right.'

Bragg snorted. 'All that education, and you are still half-witted. Three years at Cambridge; but a glimpse of an underskirt, and you lose all sense.'

'Rubbish!'

'You don't think she takes you for an ordinary City clerk, do you, with that accent? Look at your frock-coat; fine material, Savile Row cut, boots from Lobbs. Women aren't stupid, you know! She's setting her cap at you. She might just pull the trick off. She could have a good life, married to a chap who is rich and stupid. At the very least, she could bank on a present or two, before you found a new bit of stuff.'

'Bronwen is fully aware of my background,' Morton said angrily. 'Had I wished to keep it from her, which I did not, I would have had to reveal it in connection with the portrait. She was most helpful to me, in persuading her father to accept the commission.'

'That's a very grand word for copying a photograph. How much is he charging?'

'I have no idea. He will know he need not concern himself about the fee. Bronwen came with me to Alderman's Walk, to get the photograph. She will have realised that I'm not a pauper!'

Bragg stared at him in disbelief. 'It's stupid buggers like you that cause crime,' he said. 'More money than you know what to do with, and the brains of a drunken donkey! Let me tell you, lad, better men than you have ruined their lives over women like her!'

Morton glared angrily at him. 'My personal affairs are nothing to do with you,' he said.

'Oh?' Bragg demanded. 'Will it be nothing to do with me if Price and Wicks knocked off Needham, and popped him into the undertakers' van? Will it be nothing to do with me, if Price is the forger of the pictures? Will it be nothing to do with me if Bronwen Price flashed her eyes at Needham to lure him to his death?'

'That, at least, seems unlikely, after what we have heard today,' Morton said mulishly.

'I reckon I ought to get you transferred to the uniformed branch. You would be able to spend your time doffing your helmet to nurse-maids with perambulators. It's about your measure!'

'That is entirely up to you, sir!'

They spent the remainder of the journey in hostile silence.

Catherine was spending the evening at home. She was minded to reread a Jane Austen. She crossed to the bookcase. Should it be

Emma? No, *Pride and Prejudice* would chime more with her mood. She took the book and was settling herself on the sofa, when her mother came in.

'Oh, Catherine!' she exclaimed. 'I am so relieved and excited!'

'What on earth about?' Catherine asked.

'Your father says he has spoken to James Morton! He is satisfied that James will be an excellent match for you. He has an ample fortune, and you will be Lady Morton one day!'

Catherine stared angrily at her mother. 'I will not be bought and sold like a prize heifer!' she said. 'I have known all about James for years. I also know that he did propose marriage to me, and I rejected him!'

'Oh, Catherine! How can you be so thoughtless, so careless of your own welfare? You may be beautiful now, have the entrée to the Prince of Wales's circle. You may be invited to society balls at all the grand houses; meet the nobility, the rich and influential. But what will your position be in five years, when you are thirty? When your looks are beginning to fade?'

'I shall be a reporter on the *City Press*,' Catherine said frostily.

'What rubbish!' her mother retorted. 'You were only offered that post through your father's influence.'

'Perhaps. But I retain it through my own ability!'

'Your merits were not sufficient to get you the editorship of *The Lady*,' Mrs Marsden said tartly.

'That is because we live in a man's world.'

'And you will for the whole of your life, however much you strive.' Her tone became wheedling. 'Could you not be just a little nice to James?' she said. 'He is such a fine young man, so civilised and honourable.'

'Then, if you think that,' Catherine said frostily, 'you may tell my father that yesterday, in the early afternoon, I saw James Morton in Whitechapel. I followed him out of curiosity. He went to what was obviously a house of ill-fame. He knocked on the door. One of the women leaned out of an upstairs window. It was obvious that she knew him. She came downstairs into the street, she pawed at him as if she knew him well; then she took him inside with her.'

Her mother smiled at her ruefully. 'One has to overlook such things, dear,' she said. 'Men are by nature promiscuous. And, believe me, at times it can be a relief ... It is a small price to pay for security, a comfortable home, children to love and care for.'

'I would never accept such a dishonest relationship!' Catherine said haughtily.

'Oh, it is easy to be high and mighty, at your age,' Mrs Marsden said. 'But what happens in bed is not all that important . . . If you let your chance go by, you will soon be singing another tune. All your friends will be married, enjoying social occasions, parties, concerts. Travelling all over the world. And you will be excluded from it all; just because you were too proud and stupid!'

'Well,' Catherine said, with contempt in her voice, 'at least I would have preserved my integrity.'

9

When Morton got to Old Jewry, next morning, he found Bragg contentedly filling his pipe. There was no trace of the rancour of the previous evening.

'Do you think there is a painter called Mr Inspector, lad?' he asked.

'I am not aware of one,' Morton said with a smile.

'Only, we have a Constable; and I was reading that there is an American painter called Sargent. If we could find one called Inspector, we would have a full house!'

'You seem imbued with the joys of spring, sir,' Morton remarked.

'Oh, things are coming together ... I was looking in that cardboard box, we got back from Inspector Cotton.' He struck a match. 'Pick up that ruler, lad.'

Morton bent, and took the ruler in his hand. It was cylindrical, of heavy wood, with a diameter of about one and a quarter inches.

'Are you suggesting that this might have been used to kill Purvis?' Morton asked.

'It could have been. It's heavy enough, that's for sure.'

Morton found himself drawn into the theorising. 'It is possible, I suppose, that Purvis could have seen Needham examining the schedules on major insurance policies. Perhaps even the policy of the Fultons, in Winchester. When the claim came in, he might have challenged Needham, and got murdered for his pains.'

'Yes ... But how is anybody going to prove it, if that is the way it was? No witnesses. Both victim and murderer dead.'

Morton smiled. 'If that is indeed the position, Inspector Cotton will have ample justification, for once, in writing the case off as insoluble.'

The door opened and the Commissioner came in. For once he seemed optimistic and authoritative.

'I gather that you went down to the West Country, yesterday,' he said briskly.

Bragg put down his pipe. 'Yes, sir,' he said.

'In connection with the Needham case?'

'Yes, sir. We went down to Malmesbury, to the school he attended. We discovered that, while he was there, he became very friendly with a Gideon Wicks.'

'The same person who runs that Cornhill Gallery?'

'We believe so, sir.'

'I see!' Then the brief excitement faded from his face. 'So, where does this take us?' he asked.

'Well, the coroner was criticising us, because we had no provable connection between the two. Now we have this.'

'But can we act on it? How can we use it?'

Bragg smiled wryly. 'We cannot go so far as to prove Wicks killed Needham. Though that, for my money, is what happened. But we do know that Wicks is selling fake paintings.'

'Fakes?'

'Yes, sir. A Constable, a Gainsborough, a Stubbs and some Reynolds portraits.'

'I see.' Sir William frowned. 'I would want to be sure of our ground,' he said.

'Oh, there is no doubt about it, sir. We have had them examined, on the quiet, by a Royal Academician.'

'And, would he be prepared to give evidence?'

'I presume so, sir. If not, there would be plenty of art school lecturers who would jump at the chance.'

The Commissioner's face set in a resolute frown. 'Then, arrest him, sergeant!' he said.

'We would need a warrant, sir,' Bragg said briskly. 'But you can issue one on your own authority.'

A shadow of doubt crossed the Commissioner's face, to be replaced by a look of determination. 'I have rarely done so,' he said. 'But the time has come for action! In view of this Needham connection, there is ample justification for such a course. Yes, Bragg! Give me half an hour, to look up the precedents, and you shall have your warrant!'

Eleven o'clock saw Bragg and Morton pushing into the Cornhill

Gallery. Wicks was involved with a customer; there was no one else there. Morton noted that Bronwen's tapestry had been sold. The fact gave him a warm feeling of satisfaction.

The customer departed, with her parcel, and Wicks came towards them. 'Good morning, gentlemen,' he said, a look of mild puzzlement on his face.

'City police,' Bragg said gruffly.

Wicks's face cleared. 'Ah, yes. You are the officer who came about the broken window. I assure you, officer, that I had it repaired that very day!'

'It's not about the window,' Bragg said brusquely. 'We have reason to believe that you are dealing in counterfeit pictures.'

Wicks frowned. 'I do not understand you, officer,' he said.

'I mean that the pictures here are not what they seem.'

'You can demonstrate that, can you?' Wicks said coldly.

'Oh, yes.' Bragg went over to the rear wall. 'This is supposed to be by Stubbs. Right?'

'That is what the card says.'

'But, you see, we can prove it isn't.'

A supercilious smile touched Wicks's lips. 'Enlighten me, sergeant,' he said.

'That carriage is a Stanhope gig. You can tell that from the double springing.'

'If you say so.'

'Right. Now, we can prove that the vehicle could not have been made before May of 1815. But Stubbs had died in 1806.'

'I see,' Wicks said warmly. 'Thank you for pointing it out, sergeant.' He reached over and removed the name-card from the frame.

'I reckon you will have to do that to the lot, sir. They are all fakes.'

Wicks looked at him in consternation. 'Whatever grounds do you have for saying that?' he asked.

'We have had them looked at.'

'By whom?' Wicks demanded.

'By a Royal Academician. He is prepared to give expert evidence that the Constable wasn't painted by Constable, the Gainsborough isn't a genuine Gainsborough, and so on.'

Wicks looked at Bragg in puzzlement. 'I have had twenty years in the art trade, sergeant. Yet I would have taken them as authentic.'

'Oh, they are good, sir,' Bragg said warmly. 'Most people would be taken in – though whether that extends to you is a different matter.'

Wicks went over to the Gainsborough and scrutinised it. 'I cannot distinguish that painting from the many others I have seen by the artist . . . If forgery it is, it must have been done many years ago. Look at the surface cracks.'

'Yes. But I wouldn't worry about them, sir. I am told they can be produced by popping the painting into an oven. And, if you look at the Stubbs, you will see surface cracks there. But we know that is not genuine.'

'This is all very disturbing, officer,' Wicks said. 'But I still do not understand the grounds on which your so-called expert condemns the others.'

'It is a matter of technique, apparently. A Gainsborough should have a silken finish; the surface of a Constable more rough, like tapestry.'

Wicks gave an unpleasant smile. 'Well, it is hardly the place or the time to debate the matter. But I still do not understand the purpose of your visit.'

'Because you are defrauding the public, that's what.'

Wicks gave a superior smile. 'No, sergeant, neither in fact nor intent.'

'But you have got a card on every picture, saying "Stubbs" or "Constable" or "Reynolds".'

'Nevertheless, the gallery is not thereby giving any kind of warranty concerning the painter. In fact, quite the reverse.'

'What do you mean by that?' Bragg demanded.

'There is a well-understood convention in the art world. You will be able to verify this by going to any auction house. Let us take Constable as an example. If the entry in the catalogue says "John Constable", it means that in their opinion the picture is indeed by the artist. If the entry were to be "J. Constable" they are conveying their view that at least part of the work was painted by the artist. But if the catalogue merely says "Constable", it is intended to convey that the painting is by a follower of the artist, or in his style. You will note that all our attributions give the surname only.'

'But you are defrauding the public!' Bragg said angrily. 'I could come into this shop, lay out a fortune in the belief that I am buying a real Constable, and go off with something even you don't think is genuine.'

'As you must know,' Wicks said soothingly, 'the fundamental basis of every transaction of purchase and sale is *caveat emptor*. Let the buyer beware. Having indicated our view of the paintings in the traditional manner, our responsibility in the matter has been discharged.'

'No, it bloody hasn't,' Bragg said angrily. 'I have here a warrant for your arrest, for obtaining money by deception. Give the officer your keys. He will make a detailed list of every item on the premises. They will then be locked up until further notice!'

Morton spent almost two hours in listing the contents of the shop. Indeed, it would have taken considerably longer, had he noted every item of silver, china and glass separately. He saw several items of furniture that he would have liked to possess himself. 'Covet' was Catherine's word, with its titillating flavour of sin . . . He realised that he had been making assumptions that might not be valid. He had always envisaged a period when, after marriage, he would still be living in London – even continuing to serve as a policeman. Unconsciously he had assumed that he and his wife would live in the Alderman's Walk rooms; be looked after by Mr and Mrs Chambers. But that might not be the case. His wife might prefer to live in a more fashionable area, in elegant rooms in the West End, where she could entertain their friends. Indeed, that would almost certainly be the case. His father could live for fifteen, twenty years more. He would not wish such an apprenticeship on his wife, however prepared she was to ultimately become chatelaine at Ashwell Priory . . . Certainly Alderman's Walk would be no place for children. He mentally kicked himself for mawkish day-dreaming, and applied himself to finishing his list.

That done, he took the bunch of keys and began systematically to try them in the locks. As there was only one door from the street, the other keys must fit locks in the apartment upstairs. He went up to the next floor. Wicks's living quarters were by no means sumptuous. There were one or two Persian carpets in the rooms, some well-worn leather armchairs. Otherwise, the furnishings were tasteful, without being either valuable or distinguished. Hardly the Aladdin's cave he had expected to find. So, Wicks's resources did not match the pretensions of the gallery. Morton went round all the doors, trying keys in locks. Eventually, he had found a lock for every key on the bunch, except one. It did not look like a room key; for one thing, it was far too elaborate. An outside door, then. But he had already identified the key to the door of the gallery. Perhaps he should report back to Sergeant Bragg, propound his theories to him . . . No. There was no need for discussion. Either he was right, or he was wrong. And, if he were indeed wrong, he need say nothing.

He locked up the Cornhill Gallery, and set off for the warehouse in Crooked Lane. All seemed quiet. There were no vans drawn up outside. One or two pedestrians were sauntering along the street, but all was normal and peaceful. He crossed over and tried the elaborate key in the lock. It fitted! He eased open the door. Inside it appeared much the same as it had, when Tommy Skerret had picked the lock for them. The long-case clock was still there; possibly because no one had asked Wicks to obtain one for them. Morton toyed with the idea of listing the contents. But it was not a task for one person alone. And, without torches, the light coming through the grimy windows was dim indeed. He turned out of the warehouse, and locked the door after him. Then he made his way back to Old Jewry. He was feeling elated. Another piece of the jigsaw had been fitted in; a clear overall pattern was beginning to emerge.

'So, at the very least he had a key to the warehouse, eh?' Bragg said next morning. 'The way he was protesting his innocence, you would have thought he was John the Baptist!'

'We can challenge him about the clock, now,' Morton said cheerfully.

'No . . . Not yet, lad. That's the only thing we can put to him, if what he says about the pictures stands up. He could easily say he bought it. Even slip someone a couple of quid, to swear that it went through his hands. No. I would like to have some flesh on the case first. Go along to the City of London company, and the Imperial. Ask them to look through their major burglary claims, over the last five years, say. Get them to give you details of the principal pieces, that can be easily identified. We might as well get someone else doing a bit of work.'

'You do not see the key as significant?' Morton asked in surprise.

'Oh, it's significant, all right. But it's not cast-iron . . . apart from the fact that it is made of brass! No. I wouldn't want to bring it up, only to have him say a friend gave it to him, when he stored some things there, last month. If you put matters to a suspect as they arise, you fritter away your advantage.'

'I suppose so . . . Would it be too far-fetched, to link Tommy Skerret into the scenario that is emerging?' Morton asked. 'Wicks is always urging on his customers, that he can get anything they care to ask for. Suppose that a client asked him to find him a French mantel clock, with cherubs and a naked goddess.'

'Now you are being fanciful,' Bragg said.

'Not at all! House contents have still to be insured, even when they are in a repository.'

'But, would the insurance company know exactly where they were stored?'

'They might.'

'Well, you will be able to ask them, won't you? Off you go!'

Bragg finished his pipe, then went downstairs. As he neared the entrance, the desk sergeant called him over.

'That bloke of yours, in the cells, is a rum one and no mistake,' he said. 'You know how they usually go on – cursing and swearing. This Wicks chap wants to hold a debate with everybody. Protests his innocence, asks the duty-man to pop over to his solicitors with a note! I tell you what, Joe, you had better be sure of your ground.'

'Oh, the Commissioner will back me up,' Bragg said smugly. 'After all, he signed the warrant!'

Once in the street, he began to wish he had worn his overcoat. The wind blew chill from the east, as he walked along Moorgate; black clouds were obscuring the sun. The weather was on the change; was his luck about to run out, too? He reached Finsbury Circus, to find a furniture van drawn up outside the Needhams' house. The horses had nose-bags on; they would be there for a long time. Was Mrs Needham about to skedaddle? He hurried into the hallway. The stair carpet had been rolled up and placed near the door. Two men with sinewy, tattooed arms were manoeuvring a settee down the final flight of stairs.

'Is Mrs Needham around?' Bragg asked them.

'Upstairs,' one of them grunted, and pushed past him.

He found Mrs Needham in the sitting-room, gazing pensively out over the Circus. The curtains were gone, the carpet rolled up.

'Are you doing a moonlight flit?' he asked, trying to inject some humour into his voice.

'Oh, Sergeant Bragg! You startled me,' she said.

'Sorry, ma'am, I just came over for a chat.'

She twisted her mouth wryly. 'There is nowhere to talk in comfort,' she said.

'So, you are moving out?'

'Yes. This house is far too big for me. Nor is it in an area that I wish to live in. My father advised me to sell the unexpired portion of the lease, and go back to the bosom of my family. I have rented a small house in Windsor. Which means that much of the furniture will be surplus to my requirements.'

'I see.' The Constable landscape was propped against a wall. Bragg wandered over and surreptitiously looked across its surface. To him, it looked just like the so-called Constable in Wicks's shop.

'You will be selling this now, I suppose,' he said.

'Why ever would I do that?' she asked in surprise.

'I was just thinking that you have a good few years ahead of you. It must have cost your late husband a great deal of money.'

She frowned. 'Not at all, sergeant. It was given to me personally.'

'May I ask by whom, ma'am?'

'It is hardly a matter that could concern you,' she said haughtily.

'Very well, ma'am, I understand . . . It seems, reading the article in the *City Press*, that you did not have much of a time.'

She frowned. 'Whatever gave you that idea?' she asked.

'It just looked that way. You being so much younger than your husband, and having no children.'

'Not every woman wants children,' she said sharply.

'No, I suppose not . . . It seems that you came to live here soon after your marriage.'

'Two years after. In 1886.'

'So you have had nine years of it – living in an area you didn't like, away from your friends.'

'Such is the lot of many women, sergeant. Of men also. One learns to make the best of things.'

'Yes, ma'am. And now you are free to live somewhere more congenial.'

Mrs Needham did not reply.

129

'Tell me, ma'am,' Bragg said after a pause. 'Did your husband have a deed-box, or a safe in the house?'

Mrs Needham frowned. 'Not that I am aware of . . . No, I am sure he did not.'

'Only, we did not find some of the items we would have expected, in the stuff we took from his desk.'

'What would you have expected to find?' she asked. 'I know nothing about our affairs. Clifford dealt with all that.'

'Why, I would have looked to find the insurance policy relating to your household possessions, life insurance policies, and so on. Being an insurance man himself, I was sure he would have them.'

'I am sure that he did, sergeant. Indeed, my father was asking me about the life insurance policies, the other day.'

'Do you think that he might have had a deed-box deposited with the bank?' Bragg asked.

She frowned. 'I am not aware of one. If he did entrust such a box to a bank, I am sure it would be to the National Provincial's branch at Windsor.'

'I see . . . Then I might go along there. If I find anything, I will let you know . . . What will be your address in Windsor?'

'A letter sent care of Fotheringay & Phelps will reach me. That is the title of my father's accountancy practice.'

'I see,' Bragg said good-humouredly. 'And, were you a Fotheringay, or a Phelps?'

There was no answering smile. 'I was a Hawtrey, sergeant. My father is Thomas Hawtrey.'

Bragg arrived in Windsor at half-past one. He had a pork pie and a pint of yeasty beer in a pub. Promptly on two o'clock, he was standing on the pavement, as the bank unlocked its door. He marched past a protesting clerk to the manager's office, and flung open the door.

'You didn't tell me Needham had a strong-box deposited with you!' he said roughly.

The manager paled. 'I, er . . . I was not aware that he had,' he said feebly.

'Don't give me that shit! His wife says that he has. And I want to see it!'

The manager took a file from a drawer in his desk, and

consulted it briefly. Then he sidled timidly past Bragg. 'I have to get it from the vault,' he said.

Bragg stood in the doorway, watching, until the manager reappeared. He placed a rather flimsy deed-box on the desk.

'That is what you seek,' he said.

'Have you got a key?' Bragg asked.

'A key? Of course not! How could a client be assured of confidentiality, if he were to leave a key with the bank!'

'Then, have you got a lever, a screwdriver? Something we can open it with.'

The manager shook his head.

Bragg strode over to a press in the corner, and flung open the door. Its shelves were mostly filled with correspondence files and ledgers. But, at the bottom, was a miscellaneous jumble of string, ink pots, bundles of pencils. Half buried in it he saw a claw-hammer. He brandished it under the manager's nose.

'You must witness this,' he said. 'Because you will remain responsible for anything I do not take away. So you might as well help me. Get hold of that box – firmly, mind!'

Bragg managed to insert the claw of the hammer between the lid and the lip of the box. Then he levered back on the shaft. There was a crack, and the lid burst open. Inside was a miscellany of documents. Needham's birth certificate, in an envelope with his marriage certificate. A bundle of life assurance policies. An insurance policy with the Imperial company, on the contents of the Finsbury Circus house. Bragg looked rapidly through the schedule. There was a mention of a landscape painting, but no specific value was attributed to it. The amount ascribed to unspecified valuables was a mere four hundred pounds. There was a bundle of banknotes; two hundred and fifty pounds, in total. Only one envelope was left; a large manilla envelope that had once been sealed with wax. Bragg opened it, and slid out the contents. On the top was a receipt, on the headed notepaper of Sanderson & Co., of High Holborn. It recorded the receipt of fifty pounds in cash, on the twenty-seventh of October, 1894, for services rendered. Attached to the receipt were seven share certificates, each for one share in George Barber Ltd. in the names of the seven individuals shown in the official register at Somerset House.

*

Bragg had barely got back to Old Jewry, when Morton came in, a frown on his face.

'I fail to understand the logic of insurance,' he said irritably. 'No wonder burglars flourish! First of all, we find a valuable clock. We spend time and effort tracing its owner. Yet, when we tell him we have discovered it, he would prefer not to have it returned to him. Likewise, when I went to the City of London company and the Imperial, they showed not the slightest interest in looking through past claims!'

'It's all down to money, lad,' Bragg said amiably.

'So I gather! Once a claim has been paid, it is ancient history. It seems to be axiomatic that the claimant will have spent the insurance monies received. Further, the insurers have no interest in maintaining a department, merely to dispose of articles we recover, but which they have paid out on.'

'They must technically own them, though.'

'Yes. I gather that their disposal is left to the discretion of the local branch manager, or agent.'

'Hmm ... A nice little side-line for some! Anyway, I had better luck than you. Guess what I found, in Needham's bank in Windsor ... A deed-box. And, inside it, the certificates for the seven issued shares in George Barber Ltd.'

'Needham?' Morton exclaimed. 'So he was, in effect, Wicks's landlord.'

'On the surface, anyway. Whether your insurance companies co-operate or not, any fool can see what was happening. To all intents and purposes, that company was still dormant. Needham had not notified the Companies Office that he had bought the shares. He pays the rent on the Cornhill Gallery and the Crooked Lane store, to the Turbridy Estate. That keeps them happy. A perfect set-up, if you are on the fiddle!'

'And one might assume,' Morton said, 'that he was paying the rent out of the mysterious amounts of cash he was receiving.'

'That's right, lad. Which, to my mind, brings us back to Wicks. I reckon he is the spider at the centre of this web. And we have got him locked up!'

Morton frowned. 'I would accept that there is prima facie evidence, implicating Needham with whatever was going on in the Crooked Lane warehouse. But no more, surely? We might find that he has lent the premises to someone; or leased them out separately from the Cornhill Gallery.'

Bragg scowled. 'All right, lad. What do you suggest we do now? Let's have something constructive, for a change.'

There came a tap on the door, and the desk sergeant put his head in. 'Wicks's solicitor has come, Joe,' he said. 'Wants to see you.'

'Blast it! All right,' Bragg said resignedly. 'Who is he?'

'A Mr Pocklington, from Wiggins & Hulbert.'

'All right. Send him in.'

Pocklington was short and plump. His ruddy face suggested a liking for the bottle. He sat down with a weary smile.

'I understand,' he said, 'that my client, Mr Gideon Wicks, is at present incarcerated in the cells here.'

'That is correct, sir,' Bragg said evenly. 'He was arrested yesterday.'

'On what charge?'

'Selling fake pictures.'

Pocklington frowned. 'Who is your complainant?' he asked.

'We do not have a complainant, as such.'

'No complainant?'

'No, sir. But we have it, on expert authority, that pictures in his shop were not painted by the artists whose names are on the little cards.'

'Is that a crime, sergeant?'

'Offering them for sale as genuine is,' Bragg said firmly.

Pocklington frowned. 'I remember researching the point, some time ago, at my client's request. I came to the conclusion that, although the law was somewhat untidy, there was nothing criminal in what he was doing.'

'So, he consulted you about it?' Bragg said in astonishment.

'Oh, yes, sergeant. There are grey areas in the law relating to the sale of goods, I admit; but I cannot see how the criminal law encompasses them.'

'Fraud, sir. That's how we see it. The Commissioner himself signed the warrant for Wicks's arrest.'

Pocklington raised his eyebrows. 'I see,' he said. 'Well, setting aside the merits of the charge, the situation is that my client is languishing in the cells. For a man of his unblemished reputation, that is surely unnecessary. I would have thought that he could be safely released on police bail.'

Bragg frowned. 'Are you going to stand surety for him?' he asked.

Pocklington shrugged. 'That would hardly be in accord with normal practice,' he said.

'Then, it will have to wait till morning. Wicks will be coming up at the Mansion House court, at ten o'clock tomorrow morning. You can apply for bail to the magistrate then.'

When Pocklington had gone, Bragg went down to the cells. Wicks was slumped against the back wall. A night's incarceration seemed to have taken the middle-class arrogance out of him. Bragg unlocked the door of his cell and sat on the bed beside him.

'Your solicitor has just been in,' he said. 'Asking for bail, he was.'

Wicks brightened. 'Thank God!' he said. 'Can I go now?'

'You will have to see what the magistrate says, tomorrow morning. Even then, it isn't certain. If the police oppose bail, you will have to stay here.'

'But, why should they not allow it? I have not committed any crime! It is utterly intolerable that the police should behave in such an arbitrary way,' Wicks said angrily. 'I shall complain to my Member of Parliament.'

Bragg sucked in his breath. 'I will pretend that I didn't hear that,' he said censoriously. 'It sounded like you were threatening the police; when we are only doing our duty. It wouldn't do you any good in court.'

'Court?'

'Yes, sir. As I said, you will be up before the magistrate, tomorrow morning. I have informed your solicitor of the fact.'

'But I must have a barrister!' Wicks exclaimed. 'Pocklington could never argue my case properly.'

'It will not be a matter of arguing it,' Bragg said. 'Just a question of whether you should be let out on bail, pending the trial.'

Wicks winced. 'So, you intend to go on with this farce!'

'Intemperate words do you no good at all,' Bragg admonished him. 'Perhaps we ought to oppose bail, in your case.'

'But, what is to be gained by keeping me locked up here?'

'Why, sir,' Bragg said solemnly, 'we'll know where you are when we want you . . . Of course, we might consider not opposing

134

bail, if we were in a position to tell the magistrates that you were co-operating with us.'

'How on earth can I co-operate, in relation to a charge that is totally without substance?' Wicks exclaimed.

'Well, you could begin by telling us the name of the person who is painting those pictures for you.'

Wicks stared angrily at him. 'And, if I refuse?' he said.

'Why, I reckon you would be here for a long while. A fraud charge has to be tried at the Old Bailey. So all the magistrates can do, is keep you safe till your name comes up. About three months, I reckon. And it doesn't even count towards your sentence.'

Wicks's face was white. He swallowed painfully. 'It was a man I met when we were both at the Slade School of Art,' he said. 'His name is Evan Price.'

'And, how long has he been painting these pictures for you?'

'Many years now . . . Since 1892.'

'Have you heard the news about Emily?' Catherine asked Morton excitedly. They were dining in the Criterion restaurant, near Piccadilly Circus.

'Emily? What news?' Morton asked.

'Ah! I fear that I am being indiscreet!'

'Since Emily is my sister, I fail to see how you could possibly tell me anything I should not know,' Morton protested.

'But perhaps before you ought to know!'

Morton smiled. 'Come! You have gone so far, you might just as well continue.'

'Only if you promise faithfully to tell no one else!'

'Goodness me! The secrets of the confessional, eh? Very well, I promise.'

'Emily thinks that she may be pregnant, that she may be going to have a child!'

'Well, well,' Morton said grudgingly. 'So there may soon be an heir to the Smith banking dynasty. No doubt Reuben will be delighted.'

'An heir or an heiress! And the Smiths will not be the only ones who are delighted, if it is true. Emily could be producing the possible heir to the Morton family estates . . . or heiress, of course!

135

'But not an heir to the baronetcy,' Morton said sharply. 'That, at least, cannot descend through the female line.'

Catherine smiled at him. 'You seem to be less than delighted at the news,' she said teasingly.

'Not at all. I am very pleased. When the news is official, I shall certainly write to Reuben and congratulate him.'

'But not to your sister? She is, after all, much the more important participator in the enterprise!'

'To them both, of course . . . I am sorry if I sound churlish. I do not mean to be. Perhaps I have been allowing Edwin's condition to weigh too much on my mind.'

'That is perfectly natural. But now there may be something positive to set against it.'

Morton sighed. 'In a way, I feel that I opted out of my parents' anxieties by going to Australia. Now I seem to be trying to make up for it. I have even gone to the lengths of having an artist make a portrait in oils, from a photograph of Edwin, so that he can hang in the gallery with his forebears.'

'That is a kind, considerate thing to do,' Catherine said.

'Perhaps. Even so, it has a farcical aspect all of its own. I persuaded a picture restorer to do it for me. My thinking was that someone of his particular skills would be able to see beyond the photograph, and recreate Edwin at his present age, but in full vigour.'

'I see nothing farcical in that,' Catherine said warmly.

'Ah, but you see, the painter I chose has now been identified by Wicks as the artist who has faked all the old masters for him!'

'What a tangled web! And where is this artist's studio?'

'In Love Court, near Spitalfields market.'

'Ah!' Catherine said, satisfaction in her voice. 'Then, since it is confession time, let me unburden myself of something I found most provoking.'

'Provoking?' Morton asked with a smile. 'It can have nothing to do with me. I would never have the audacity to provoke you.'

'But you did. Indirectly, perhaps, but I was quite vexed!'

'That sounds almost like a line from a Restoration comedy! However, if I have in any way offended you, please give me the opportunity to set the matter right.'

'It is not possible, for it was not something that you did, so much as what you said.'

'Words are ephemeral. In a breath they are gone, as if they had never been uttered.'

Catherine frowned. 'That belittles me even more,' she said.

'Belittles you?' Morton said in astonishment.

'Yes, belittles me. You had a conversation with my father, last Sunday.'

'Indeed. I was awaiting your august presence!'

'As I understand it, I was the subject of this conversation.'

'Only indirectly, I assure you,' Morton said with a smile.

'It is not indirect, to haggle over me with my father, as if I were a prize heifer!'

'A prize, certainly, but one to be cherished, not diminished. In any case, it was your father who began the conversation.'

'And, are you suggesting that I should be any the less provoked, because of that?' Catherine asked.

10

Friday morning saw Bragg and Morton striding down the streets of Whitechapel, to Love Court. Morton knocked on the door of the Prices' house. After several minutes an upper window was opened, and the tousled head of Bronwen appeared.

'James!' she called in surprise. 'Just a minute. I'll let you in.'

The policemen waited for considerably longer than a minute. Morton uncharitably wondered who was being let out of the back door. Then Bronwen appeared, her hair tidied, a crisp cotton blouse tucked into her smart wool skirt.

'I did not expect you so early, James,' she said reproachfully. 'Come in.'

They followed her up the stairs to her father's studio.

'There!' Bronwen said. 'It's finished! But be careful. Some of the paint will not be fully dry.'

Morton picked up the portrait. It was uncanny! Edwin stared out at him with his old self-assurance, his arrogant assumption that the world was his oyster. A more mature Edwin than that in the photograph; but still very much his elder brother. The effect was unpleasantly startling. Morton began to wonder about the wisdom of the enterprise. His parents might well be delighted. But would he himself be content to have those eyes sardonically watching him every day, when he inherited Ashwell Priory? Well, that was a problem for another time.

The door opened and Evan Price came in. He, too, had obviously just crawled from his bed.

'Do you like it?' he asked. 'Was that what you had in mind?'

'It is remarkable,' Morton said. 'I am exceedingly grateful to you. How much do I owe you?'

Price smiled. 'I said I would leave you and Bronwen to settle that between you.'

Morton pulled out his notecase and took out a hundred-pound note. He pressed it into Bronwen's hand. 'I hope this will be enough,' he said.

Her eyes opened wide, and a delighted smile touched her lips, then faded.

'I never meant you to pay for it,' she said. 'Not like this, anyway.'

'I am afraid I have to tell you,' Morton said quietly, 'that I am a police officer. This is my superior, Sergeant Bragg.'

'Bastard!' Bronwen spat the word out like an angry snake.

Her father seemed unperturbed. 'What do you want of us?' he asked.

Bragg cleared his throat. 'I have to tell you,' he said, 'that we are aware of your connection with the Cornhill Gallery. The proprietor, Mr Gideon Wicks, has been arrested on a charge of selling counterfeit old master paintings, with intent to defraud the public.'

'So?'

'He has identified you as the faker of those paintings.'

'Faker?' Price echoed. 'I never faked a painting in my life! I'm not having that!'

'Very well,' Bragg said patiently. 'He has paintings in his shop . . .'

'Gallery,' Price interrupted with a smile. 'He doesn't like people to call it a shop!'

'It will do for me! He has pictures in his shop with cards on. We can prove that they were not painted by the artist whose name is on the card. In my book, that is fraudulent.'

'Even if that is so, it is Wicks who is selling them. Anyway, how do you know he is telling the truth about them being fakes? Are the police experts about paintings all of a sudden?'

'It was the Stubbs. You painted the couple sitting in a carriage that was not even designed until nine years after Stubbs died.'

Price laughed. 'Now, my wife would never have made a mistake like that! Thorough she was.'

'So, do you admit it?' Bragg demanded.

'Admit what? That I got the Stubbs wrong?'

'That you forged it!'

'But I didn't.'

'Then who did?'

139

Price shook his head. 'No, you've got it wrong. There was never any question of passing them off as real. I was doing original paintings in the styles of various old masters. I have a flair for it, see. I used to do it at the Slade, to amuse the lads.'

· 'You are not doing it for art students now,' Bragg said roughly.

'No. I get paid now! Not much; but enough to keep the wolf from the door.'

'So you know that Wicks is selling the pictures you paint, as genuine old masters?'

Price frowned. 'No. What's more, I don't believe he is. There is a big market for what I call furnishing pictures. These newly rich industrialists in the Midlands and the North. They build great mansions in the shadow of their factories, yet want people to think they have been there for centuries. All I do is meet the demand.'

'You supply Wicks's need for paintings he can pass off as old. You even bake them to get the surfaces to crack!'

'What if I do?' Price asked. 'It's all part of the illusion. You are not telling me that anybody is fool enough to think they are getting a genuine Gainsborough, for the prices Wicks charges?'

'So you know what he is asking?'

'I know what he pays me; I know he says he cannot afford to give me more.'

'So it comes down to this. You paint pictures in the style of an old master, at the request of Gideon Wicks, knowing full well he will put them in his shop with that painter's name on.'

Price frowned. 'Steady on,' he said. 'What happens is that he will ask me to do a painting of, say, a young courtier in the style of Vandyke. I knock it off, he pays me a few quid; that's the end of it as far as I am concerned. I am not copying any existing painting – which would be forgery, I suppose. I am just creating an original painting of my own, but in the style of another painter. I never sign my paintings. I certainly never try to copy the signature of the master I am following.'

'But you must be aware,' Bragg said roughly, 'that Wicks puts little cards on the frame with the names of those painters.'

'That's no concern of mine. I just carry out his instructions. What he does when he gets the pictures, is up to him.'

'In our view, you have entered into a criminal conspiracy with Wicks to defraud the public.'

'Rubbish!' Price said angrily. 'No one who knows anything

140

about art could possibly be taken in. All you have to do is look across the surface of the paintings. It's obvious that my prospects in the style of Constable were not painted by him. I could not reproduce his technique, even if I tried.'

'It wouldn't be obvious to me,' Bragg said. 'Or to ninety-nine per cent of the public. Get your coat on. I am arresting you for conspiracy to defraud.'

'You rotten swine!' Bronwen screeched. She darted forward and struck Morton across the cheek.

'Don't you worry, love,' Price said calmly. 'You can use some of that hundred pounds to get me a lawyer.'

Bragg had no sooner charged Price, and seen him locked in a cell close to Wicks's, than he received a summons from the coroner. He pulled out his watch. It was already past noon. There was no point in going now, and have Sir Rufus itching to get away to lunch at some livery company or other. Instead, he and Morton wandered along Cheapside, to have a leisurely lunch in a pub by St Paul's churchyard.

'Have you still got Wicks's keys, lad?' Bragg asked.

'Yes. Why?'

'I was thinking it might be a good idea if we had a more detailed list of all these faked old masters.'

'Of course! We shall certainly need more information than we already have, to frame charges. I will go after lunch.'

'Better than being put through the mincer by the coroner! Now, then, what's on the slate for today?'

By two o'clock Bragg was seated in the waiting room of Sir Rufus Stone's chambers. The only other person there was a middle-aged man with a gaunt face and tired eyes. He hardly looked prosperous enough to afford a consultation with a top-rate barrister. But, then again, he might merely be the clerk of a not very thriving solicitor. Bragg's speculations were interrupted by the entrance of the coroner.

'Come!' he said to Bragg, as he swept by.

Bragg sat down at the coroner's desk, his eyes on a Hogarth print opposite the window. Sir Rufus took up his favourite position a-straddle the fireplace, one hand holding the lapel of his morning coat.

141

'Well, Bragg?' he said belligerently. 'What is this I hear about my officers running amok; recklessly incarcerating innocent citizens?'

'Not reckless, sir,' Bragg said stolidly.

'Yes, reckless! Caring nothing for the repercussion! I am not amused to have it bruited abroad that my designated officer is being high-handed. Acting without regard to the provisions of the law which governs this great country of ours.'

'I would never be party to anything illegal,' Bragg said piously. 'Though the law is sometimes a bit obscure.'

'Ignorance is no defence, as you well know! I gather that, yesterday, you arrested Wicks, of that gallery in Cornhill. What was the charge?'

'Fraud, sir.'

'Huh! The term is a catch-all. What are the fraudulent acts complained of?'

'We do not have a complainant, as such,' Bragg said. 'But we do have this man Wicks selling pictures to the public, with cards that have names on them – Constable, Stubbs, Gainsborough and so on. This morning we have interviewed the man who painted them.'

'Ah! You have obtained a confession from him?'

'Oh, yes, sir. He is making out that he has done nothing wrong – even though he knew Wicks was putting these misleading cards on them.'

'The name of this painter?' Sir Rufus demanded.

'Price. Evan Price. A Welshman.'

'That last fact had communicated itself to my overburdened brain,' the coroner said sarcastically. 'And are you contending that this Welsh painter has been defrauding someone?'

'The public, sir.'

'That term is an abstract, Bragg. You can not arraign someone at the bar of justice, on the grounds that some class or coterie of unspecified individuals has been injured by the accused. You have to be precise.'

'What about forgery, sir?' Bragg asked.

Sir Rufus wrinkled his nose. 'That essentially relates to deception by writing, or in written instruments. I suppose one might extend it to a false signature or sign, placed upon a painting.'

'Price never put a signature on his fakes, sir.'

'It is tendentious to use such a term,' the coroner reproved him. 'Please keep an open mind.'

'Yes, sir. What about perjury?'

'Out of the question, Bragg. It can only be committed by swearing a falsehood during criminal proceedings . . . So far as Wicks is concerned, one might consider a charge for false pretences. But that must fail as between Wicks and Price, because the former procured the creation of these pictures. What is the situation regarding Wicks?'

'We charged him with fraudulent trading, yesterday. He was given bail this morning.'

Sir Rufus pondered. 'Well, you have a marginally better case, so far as he is concerned, since he was actually selling these pictures to the public. It will all depend on the nature of the representations made to the buyers. But you will find the doctrine of *caveat emptor* a formidable hurdle.'

'We do have the robbery-to-order business, still. We could throw that at Wicks.'

'Have you obtained convincing evidence of that? Or are you still in the realms of speculation?'

'Not exactly evidence – not for Wicks, anyway. But the landlord of both the Cornhill Gallery and the Crooked Lane warehouse is a company named George Barber Ltd. Yesterday I found the certificates for all the issued shares. They were in a deed-box owned by Clifford Needham.'

'But Needham is dead.'

'Yes, sir. But it does show there was a connection between Needham and the shady goings-on at the Cornhill Gallery.'

'A somewhat tenuous one, at best. Who are the directors of this Barber company?'

'They are still the employees of the company-monger that set it up.'

'Surely they resigned, when the company was sold?'

'If they did resign,' Bragg said irritably, 'they did not bother to inform the Registrar of Companies. Nor did Needham.'

Sir Rufus mused. 'It is a lax area of administration,' he said, 'though the law itself is perfectly clear. It is the commercial aspects of a company's activities that muddy the waters.'

'Of course, sir.'

'At all events we have Wicks charged, and Price in the process of being charged. We are at least demonstrating that we are not completely inactive. That ought to reassure the public somewhat.'

'Not if the magistrates give them bail as soon as we arrest them,' Bragg said sourly. 'I expect that Price will be freed, too, before long.'

11

Bragg slept badly, and woke up next morning feeling dull and lethargic. To make matters worse, Dora Jenks was bustling around, chattering brightly to him as she made his breakfast.

'We ought to go before it breaks,' she asserted.

'What's that?'

'The weather, of course!'

'Oh. Go where?'

'You've not been listening to a word, Mr Bragg!' she said peevishly. 'I was saying we could have a trip to Southend, this afternoon, while the fine weather lasts. Have some oysters, while there is still an R in the month.'

'That would be nice,' Bragg said non-committally.

'Well, you usually have Saturday afternoons off. We could be there by three.'

'This afternoon? . . . Well, I suppose I might just manage it.'

'You might just?' Mrs Jenks said wrathfully. 'What's the good of being a sergeant, if you can't have time off when you want?'

'There are one or two levels above mine,' Bragg said mildly.

'I bet they are not working on a Saturday afternoon!'

'Well, I will try . . . But I have this awkward case.'

'You always have some excuse! Last year we were going to go half a dozen times. It was October, before we managed it. And it was so cold you got pleurisy!'

It was worse than being married, Bragg thought. All the shrewishness and none of the compensations. He promised to get back by one o'clock, if he could, and escaped from the house.

'Good morning!' Morton greeted him, when he arrived at Old Jewry. 'What a marvellous morning! A week or two more, like this, and we can get down to some serious cricket practice!'

'Can't you think of anything else but bloody cricket?' Bragg said irritably. 'You are like a big kid! You've just got back from three months of it; now you are itching to start again.'

'Only within the terms of the agreement I have with the Commissioner,' Morton said lightly.

'Huh! He may be satisfied. He may think he gets a better class of recruit, because they all think they will get like Jim Morton. But it's no good to me!' He held up his hand to still Morton's protests. 'I'll tell you what's wrong with this bloody Needham case, lad. You came on it half-way through. You haven't got the background; you haven't lived the case. So we are working at odds, not as a team.'

'Well, sir,' Morton said stiffly, 'if you feel you would prefer me to . . .'

There came a rap on the door, and the desk sergeant came in. 'You still on the Needham case, Joe?' he asked.

'If I'm not, nobody has bothered to tell me,' Bragg said in a disgruntled voice.

'Only, there is a bloke wanting to speak to somebody about it.'

'Oh, well,' Bragg said resignedly. 'Send him in.'

Bragg and Morton preserved an angry silence. Then there came a knock at the door, and Pocklington entered. He was wearing a frock-coat and carrying a top-hat. So, even on a Saturday morning, he observed the professional niceties.

'Has my client been rearrested?' he asked sharply.

'Wicks, you mean?'

'Of course!'

Bragg frowned. 'Not to my knowledge,' he said.

'I obtained his release, on bail, yesterday,' Pocklington said. 'He was supposed to be at my chambers at half-past eight this morning. I came in especially early to meet him; but he did not arrive. After waiting for half an hour, I began to wonder if he had been rearrested.'

'Perhaps he over-slept, or just forgot about it,' Bragg said helpfully.

'That is hardly likely! But, in the event, I went to seek him. It is important that I should establish certain facts for counsel. However, when I arrived at the Cornhill Gallery, it was still closed. I banged on the door, but no one came. I shouted but obtained no response. I therefore concluded that you must, indeed, have arrested him again.'

Bragg frowned. 'That's queer,' he said, then turned to Morton. 'You had Wicks's keys, didn't you, constable?'

'I gave them back to the desk sergeant, sir.'

Bragg got up. 'Well, let's go and look into it, shall we?' he said.

The desk sergeant asserted that Wicks had collected all his belongings, and proffered his signature as proof. In response to the alarm on Pocklington's face, Bragg suggested that they should all go to the Cornhill Gallery and try to rouse Wicks. When they arrived, the shop was still closed. Bragg hammered on the door . . . Silence. They went round the corner to Change Alley, and shouted in unison. Still no response.

'You are sure he ought to be here?' Bragg asked. 'He might have spent the night somewhere else – might be waiting at your office, even now.'

'That is hardly likely, sergeant,' Pocklington said. 'My client was, I believe, very much a creature of habit. But, in any case, I left instructions with my clerk that, should he arrive, someone should come after me.'

'Hmm . . . Well, you have a decision to make,' Bragg said. 'Either we all go home, and try again after the weekend, or we break in now.'

Pocklington hesitated. 'As his lawyer, it is hardly within my function,' he said. 'But as a fellow human being . . . After all, he may be lying sick in his bed, unable to respond to our knocking . . . Very well. You have my authority to break in.'

'In that case,' Bragg said with a grim smile, 'I reckon this window is the favoured place. Break the pane that has just been puttied in, constable. You will be able to reach the catch from there.'

When Morton had crawled through the aperture, Bragg and Pocklington went round to Cornhill. Morton was just opening the street door.

'Any sign of him, constable?' Bragg asked.

'Not on my path from the kitchen to here!'

'Then, pop upstairs. See if he is in his apartment.'

They waited by the door until Morton came clattering back. 'There is no sign of him, sir,' he said. 'There are the remains of a cold meal in the living-room, an empty wineglass. But his bed has either been made this morning, or not slept in.'

'Maybe he went out last night,' Bragg said. 'Anyway, I suppose we ought to look around here.'

Bragg was grunting with the effort of moving a big chest that was placed across one corner of the gallery, when he heard a shout from Morton at the other end. He hurried down to him. In the middle of a group of drawing-room furniture, lying on a Chinese carpet, was the body of Wicks. He was on his back, his mouth half-open, his eyes staring. Spreading from under his body was a congealing area of blood, soaked into the carpet.

'God Almighty!' Bragg exclaimed.

'It would appear that he has been shot,' Morton said. 'There is a small tear in his waistcoat, over his heart.'

Bragg knelt down and peered at the hole. 'There seems to be a powder burn, too, as if he was shot at close range,' he said. 'Well, it seems straightforward enough. Go and get the pathologist, will you, lad. And you had better leave a note at the coroner's chambers. I don't expect we shall find him there, on a Saturday morning.'

Morton strode off, and Bragg began to go through Wicks's pockets. He was stiffening, that was for sure, and cool to the touch. So he had not been murdered recently. His notecase held upwards of twenty pounds, his gold watch was still in his waistcoat pocket. Not robbery, then.

'I, er . . . I really feel that I am of no assistance here,' Pocklington said. His face was as white as Wicks's, he was blinking nervously.

'I wouldn't say that, sir,' Bragg said warmly. 'You are his legal representative, after all. It could be useful to you, to know how we found him, what condition the body was in, and so on. It's not often that a lawyer has the opportunity to see the murder scene fresh, as it were.'

'I much prefer to deal with death in the abstract,' Pocklington said. 'I find this utterly shocking.'

'Nevertheless, sir, with so much valuable stuff around, I am happier with you here . . . Where would he have kept yesterday's takings, for instance?'

Pocklington looked up in puzzlement. 'You think he was shot for . . . for a few hundred pounds?' he asked.

'Happens all the time,' Bragg said cheerfully. 'You have to remember that, not half a mile from here, are thousands of people who haven't got a few hundred ha'pennies.'

148

'Well, he had a safe in the little room off the kitchen.'

'Show me.'

Pocklington seemed relieved to be leaving the murder scene. Bragg followed him to the kitchen. The solicitor drew back a curtain screening a narrow, windowless room off it. At the far end of it was a substantial safe. Bragg went back into the showroom, and took Wicks's keys from his pocket. One by one he tried them in the lock. Eventually there was a click, and he could swing open the door. In the dim light from the kitchen, it was evident that the two top shelves were full of small objects, wrapped in tissue paper. Bragg took one out and unwrapped it. It was a small figure of a man, in greenish stone. He was squatting on his haunches, his arms folded in front of him. He showed it to the lawyer.

'I wonder why he bothered to put stuff like this in the safe,' he said, 'while there are little silver pieces left in the showroom.'

Pocklington took it from him. He seemed happier, now that he had got away from Wicks's corpse. 'This is jade,' he said. 'It is extremely valuable.'

Bragg snorted. 'I can't say that I would want it on my mantelpiece,' he said. 'There are scores of them here.'

'I recall my client saying that he collected jade figurines,' Pocklington said. 'But I had no idea that he did so on such a scale.'

'Are you saying that Wicks was a wealthy man?'

'Indeed, sergeant.'

'But, whoever killed him either didn't know, or didn't care. After all, the key to the safe was in his pocket.'

The lawyer pursed his lips. 'I suppose that must follow ... In which case, one could argue that whoever killed him did not know him very well.'

Bragg grunted his assent, then took a bundle of documents from the bottom of the safe. They were tied with pink ribbon. He tossed them to Pocklington. 'Here,' he said. 'These are more in your line than mine. What are they about?'

The lawyer undid the tape and scanned through the documents. 'This is the lease of these premises,' he said. 'And the insurance policy for the business ... Oh, and a personal life insurance policy with the Prudential.'

'How much for?'

'Five hundred pounds.'

'Is that worth killing for?'

'Hardly. Though it could depend on the financial circumstances of his legatees . . . Ah! Here is his will.'

'Did you draw it up for him?' Bragg asked.

'No. I see that it bears the name of Truelove & Smith . . . Now, I wonder why he parted company from them . . . It was made in January 1881. That was the year in which he opened this business.'

'Interesting,' Bragg remarked. 'And who gets the bunce?'

Pocklington unfolded the document, and glanced through the copper-plate paragraphs. 'I see . . .' he murmured. 'Most interesting . . . Under the terms of this will, the whole of my client's estate is bequeathed to a Clifford Needham.'

'But he was murdered too!' Bragg exclaimed. 'Less than a fortnight ago.'

'I see . . .' Pocklington turned back to the will. 'In that case, everything goes to the Slade School of Art, to found a scholarship.'

'Huh!' Bragg said grumpily. 'I can't see that lot knocking him off his perch.'

There came a banging at the outer door. Bragg went to let Morton in. 'Did you see Professor Burney?' he asked.

'No, sir. He was lecturing to his students at Bart's. But Noakes undertook to get a message to him. A van will be here, any moment, to take the body to the mortuary. Noakes suggests that we should go to Golden Lane, about three o'clock this afternoon. He is sure the pathologist will have completed his examination by then.'

'Bugger me!' Bragg said irritably. 'And Mrs Jenks is expecting me to take her to Southend! I had better go and break the news, or there will be hell to pay!' He tossed Wicks's bunch of keys to Morton. 'Here, lad,' he said. 'Make a detailed record of every one of those jade figurines in the safe. We don't want anyone accusing the police of mislaying things! Oh, and get somebody to mend that window again!'

On the stroke of three o'clock, Bragg and Morton passed through the mortuary, into Burney's examination room. The pathologist was standing at the bench under the window, poking with a probe at a grisly red mass.

'Ah!' he said, his loose mouth sagging open in delight. 'You arrive at an opportune moment . . . You have had lunch, I take it?'

150

'Yes, sir,' Bragg said hastily.

'Because there are some sandwiches over there ... Perhaps Constable Morton? ... No? Very well. You have come about this subject,' he said, gesturing to the mutilated body on his slab.

'If that is Wicks, yes.'

Professor Burney's face became oddly bashful. 'In this job,' he said, 'one sees violent death in all its forms. One is sometimes led to conjecture; to say, "If I were involved in an accident, injured unto death, how would I prefer it to be?" There is, of course, a wide variety of answers.'

'Sudden and certain, for me,' Bragg said.

'Yes. But our friend on the slab might run you a close second.'

Bragg raised his eyebrows. 'I would not have thought it all that quick,' he said.

'No. But perhaps with very little pain.' He crossed over to the recumbent corpse, and Bragg could see that the chest had been cut open along the breast-bone. Burney picked up a probe.

'He was killed by a bullet which entered between the fourth and fifth rib, on the left side of the chest.' He pushed the probe into a neat round hole in the skin. 'Like this,' he said.

'What sort of bullet?' Bragg asked.

'I would say a small-calibre revolver, or some such ... And, of course, it was fired from close range. You are aware of the gunpowder residues on the jacket?'

'Yes, sir.'

'Good. I will let you have the projectile, in due course.' Burney turned back to his bench and poked at the bloody mass of flesh with his probe. 'This is the anterior surface of the heart, and you can see the entry point of the bullet. I am about to dissect it. So you will be able to see precisely what has happened.'

'I'm sorry, sir,' Bragg said firmly. 'I have to see a suspect.'

'Ah. A pity!' Burney beamed in Morton's direction. 'Perhaps the constable would care to observe ...'

'I shall have to be with Sergeant Bragg, sir,' Morton interrupted. 'As a witness.'

The pathologist's smile dimmed. 'Ah, well. Another time,' he said. 'Then, you will have to work on my assumption of what I shall find.'

'Your assumption is preferable to anybody else's assertion,' Bragg said warmly.

Burney beamed. 'Thank you, sergeant,' he said. 'Well, there is no point of exit; so I am confident that the bullet will be in the heart. Now, its trajectory is slightly upward. If I insert my probe . . . yes, I can feel it. The bullet will have damaged the tricuspid valve of the heart. That would not cause immediate death. Rather, the life of the subject would ebb away as blood was lost from the system.'

'God! And you wouldn't mind dying that way?' Bragg exclaimed.

'Well, it would not be exceedingly painful. One would have time to consider one's misdeeds, perhaps even atone for them. Then one would simply fall asleep, as it were.'

'We certainly found Wicks lying in a pool of blood. But, are you saying that the wound would have disabled him? That he could not have got up and sought help?'

Burney gave a sheepish smile. 'That is more in your field than mine. After all, the subject might have considered that any such attempt would have invited yet another bullet. From a strictly medical view, it would have been possible for him to move for a short time; though that itself would depend on both the subject's physique and his will-power. But, after a significant amount of blood had been lost, that would have no longer been possible.'

'I see, sir . . .' Bragg pondered awhile, then: 'And, when do you think it happened?' he asked.

'I can tell you with a fair degree of accuracy when he died. But you cannot take that as more than a guide as to when he was attacked.'

'So, when did he die?'

'Around eleven o'clock last night.'

'And, could it have been suicide?'

Burney pursed his lips. 'Without having the weapon, and carrying out various tests, I cannot give you a firm answer, sergeant. But, in view of the powder burns, it seems entirely possible.'

'Then, in that case,' Bragg muttered, 'who took the gun?'

'We can confidently exclude one possibility from our rogues gallery,' Morton said. 'Evan Price was safely locked up in the Old Jewry cells at eleven o'clock last night.'

*

152

'What time is it, lad?' Bragg asked. They were sitting in a pub in Paternoster Row.

Morton pulled out his gold half-hunter. 'Almost four o'clock, sir.'

Bragg put down his glass, and wiped the foam from his moustache. 'Since Mrs Jenks and I were supposed to be going to Southend this afternoon,' he said, 'if I get home earlier than six o'clock, she will skin me alive!'

'For my part, sir,' Morton said, 'I would welcome the opportunity to prowl around the Cornhill Gallery again, while it is still light.'

Bragg cocked his head. 'Have you something in mind?' he asked.

'Nothing specific. But, since our visit this morning, I have had a vague sense of unease.'

'Then, why not?' Bragg said. 'It will suit us both.'

Once away from St Paul's, the streets were deserted. A few sightseers were gazing at the Mansion House and the Royal Exchange. An occasional cab came trotting by, the driver alert for custom. It might just as well have been Sunday, Bragg thought. They turned into Cornhill, and Morton unlocked the door of Wicks's shop. It seemed strange; quiet and chill. There was an all-enveloping silence. Bragg looked towards the place where Wicks had died. It was in full view of one of the big windows. There must have been light in the shop, from the street lamps, at near midnight. But precious few passers-by. And the light would not have illuminated the spot where Wicks's body had lain. It would be a fair chance to take; long odds against getting caught. Just sneak out of the door, and away.

Morton was wandering about, a vacant expression on his face. He went into the kitchen, then came out again. He caught Bragg's eye and shrugged apologetically. Bragg himself went over to the bloodstained carpet. Wicks had fallen backwards . . . but that was no sure guide. Had the gun been of heavy calibre, it would certainly have knocked him straight back. But he had been killed by a small-calibre bullet. He could have staggered about a bit, before collapsing. Not that there was any blood, except on the carpet . . . Anyway, it might not have been a revolver. It could have been one of those Continental automatics. In which case, there ought to be an empty cartridge case around somewhere.

153

Bragg got down on his hands and knees, and scanned the polished surface of the floor . . . He could not see one. But then, he had no idea of how far the gun would throw it. He scrabbled across the floor, towards the back wall. There was something under that bookcase . . . He pushed his arm into the narrow aperture. He could touch it with his fingers, but he could not get hold of it. Certainly it was not an empty cartridge case. It had bulk and weight. He marched past a preoccupied Morton, and took the poker from the kitchen. This was plenty long enough. He pushed it under the bookcase and swept it sideways. There was a metallic sound, and an object went skidding across the floor. Bragg got to his feet and picked it up. It was a small revolver, with a short barrel and cross-hatched butt. More of a toy than a serious weapon. But it had probably seen off Wicks.

'Come and look at this,' he called.

Morton took the revolver and weighed it in his hand. 'Beautifully made,' he said. 'And it has a nice feel to it. So, this is the murder weapon?' he said.

'Until somebody proves different, we will assume so. Professor Burney said it was a small-calibre gun. I reckon this fits the bill.'

'But, why leave it at the scene of the crime?' Morton asked. 'Why not take it away?'

Bragg shrugged. 'Not all criminals act sensibly,' he said. 'Anyway, we might as well let the pathologist have a look at it . . . Get one of those mats, over there, and drop it across the blood-stain. It will be more seemly then.'

Morton went to the back of the gallery, and gave a cry of surprise. 'This is it!' he said. 'This is what I must have seen!'

'What are you on about?' Bragg asked tetchily.

'The painting on the sofa! It is the very one that Evan Price was cleaning, when I visited his studio. We had a discussion about that white blob. He was right, it is a flower.'

'So, where does that get us?'

'It was not here, yesterday, when I listed the Price fakes! Which means that it must have been brought here since I left.'

'But you locked up, surely?'

'Indeed!'

'Well, somebody else must have a key to the place. I wonder who the hell it is.'

A shadow came over Morton's face. He frowned, staring out of

154

the window. Then he spoke in a subdued voice. 'Bronwen Price has a key to the gallery,' he said. 'She locked the door after us, when she took me to her father's studio.'

Bragg stayed silent, staring at him incredulously.

'She must have brought the painting back, after her father was charged,' Morton went on. 'Perhaps last night. How utterly stupid I have been!'

'Are you saying that she killed Wicks?' Bragg asked.

'Why not? If that revolver is the murder weapon, it could easily be hidden in a woman's coat.'

'But why would she leave it behind?'

'How can we tell? Panic, perhaps.'

Bragg sniffed. 'It's possible, I suppose. Yet, what had she to gain from killing Wicks?'

'I have no idea. Perhaps to protect her father. If Wicks could no longer be charged with selling fraudulent pictures, there would be little point in charging her father with creating them.'

'It makes a sort of sense,' Bragg said slowly. 'All right. Let's see what madam has to say for herself.'

They hurried to Whitechapel, picking their way through the crowds of people thronging the streets. Children were playing ball, in Love Court, as they approached the house where the Prices lived. Bragg hammered on the door. After some minutes, a thin, pale-faced girl opened it.

'Who do you want?' she asked suspiciously.

'Evan Price,' Bragg said quietly.

'They've gone.'

'Gone? Where have they gone?'

'I dunno,' she said.

'When did they go?'

'Sometime this morning.'

Morton burst past her and clattered up the stairs. When Bragg caught up with him, he was peering into the rooms. The furniture and curtains were there, but there was no sign of personal possessions.

'They damn well have gone!' Bragg said savagely. 'Bloody magistrates! They are shit-scared of refusing bail, nowadays!'

Morton led the way into the room that had served Price as a studio. The sofa was still there, but the easel had gone. In the corner was a pile of old canvases. Beside them, propped against

155

the wall, was the painting of the nude woman which had so roused his baser passions.

'Bloody hell!' Bragg exclaimed, following him into the room.

Morton grinned. 'She is rather fetching, isn't she?'

'Fetching be buggered!' Bragg gazed at the painting. 'Would you say that was painted from life, lad?'

Morton considered. 'Almost certainly,' he said. 'There is such vitality, such ardour, such . . .'

'Lust?' Bragg suggested.

'Well, physical passion, anyway.'

'Yes . . . Now you will understand what I meant, when I said we were working at odds . . . The woman who modelled for that picture happens to be Clifford Needham's widow.'

'Good God!' Morton exclaimed in disbelief.

'You knew the Prices well,' Bragg said sardonically. 'Where would they have done a bunk to?'

'Why, Cardiff, I suppose. That is their home city. They have relatives there – Monmouth Street.'

'Right. Telegraph the Cardiff police to look out for them. Tell them we have a warrant for their arrest. It will be true of the father, at least.'

Morton sent off the telegraph, went to his rooms for a thick overcoat, then strolled back to Old Jewry. He wanted to be there at the very moment that anything was heard from Cardiff. A duty officer was at the desk. He greeted him genially. But Morton would not be drawn into conversation. He went to Bragg's room to while away the time and think. There was substance to Bragg's criticisms of him; he had to admit that. Of course, the sergeant had been angry, felt let down. That in itself was condemnation enough, between members of a team. And it was unreasonable – arrogant even – to act as if being a policeman was something to do where there was nothing more exciting to beckon him. He thought of his fellow England cricketers. The few men of leisure did not pretend to be anything else. They paraded their masculine airs like peacocks or rutting stags. He was often secretly exultant when their arrogance was dented by a rash stroke or a brilliant catch. Thinking through the touring party, he had to acknowledge that the members he had admired and liked were the businessmen and members of professions; particularly those with families. They had a relaxed confidence in themselves. Playing cricket for England was a distinction, an honour, but it was not the substance of their life. And therein lay the rub. For himself, neither policing nor cricket were at the core of his life. To that extent Bragg's exasperated gibe was painfully accurate. He was playing at being a policeman.

But it went deeper than that. There was an element of pettiness in his behaviour. Knowing that his future must lie at the Priory, he resented having to wait. He was refusing to take third place behind an ageing father and an invalid brother; mentally stamping his foot and demanding his birthright now ... except that it was only his heritage because of Edwin's mortal wound. As an image it was repellent, despicable. He felt deeply ashamed. Yet, what was to be done? ... For a start, he ought to be more content with the present, not be looking always to the future. He could stop erecting hurdles in his mind, that would have to be jumped before he would be content. He could live for the present, not in tetchy anticipation of the future. Perhaps, in Sergeant Bragg's terms, he could concentrate on being a real policeman, and stop playing at it. He smiled to himself. Well, this was being a real policeman, in all conscience – sitting in an empty office in the middle of the night, waiting for news of runaway suspects! He carried his armchair to the corner of the room, leaned back with his head to the wall and went to sleep.

He was wakened by someone shaking his shoulder. It was the duty officer.

'Telegraph for you, Jim, from Cardiff,' he said.

Morton tore open the envelope. The Prices had been arrested as they left the train and were now in police custody. Elated, Morton scribbled a reply and set off for the telegraph office. He would be able to get a few hours' real sleep after all.

At three o'clock on Sunday afternoon Morton presented himself at the main police station in Cardiff. The woman prison officer he had requested was already there. She was big-boned, deep-chested, and had a vindictive cast to her face. Morton signed the release documents and the Prices were brought up from the cells. Bronwen's lip curled in scorn as she saw him.

'Bastard!' she hissed.

'You will both be taken back to London, where you will face serious charges,' he said pompously.

It was something of an anticlimax, to then go out into the street in search of a cab. Eventually he found one and was driven back to the police station. The wardress casually handcuffed Bronwen to her. She was obviously experienced in these matters. Morton borrowed a pair from the duty officer, and closed one end round his left wrist. Price tolerantly held out his arm and they were linked together. Throughout the short journey to the railway station Bronwen was glaring at him resentfully. The wardress took no heed of her. She gazed balefully out of the window at the afternoon traffic, occasionally muttering under her breath. When they arrived at the station she commandeered the first-class waiting room. She ejected the two elderly gentlemen who were in possession, telling them that the prisoners were killers of the blackest hue. They departed with alacrity, casting anxious glances over their shoulders.

When the train pulled into the platform, the wardress marched with her charge to a first-class compartment. There was no point in being uncomfortable, she asserted. Besides, she was having to come back again. The wardress dragged Bronwen into the train, though she showed no sign of resisting. With such Amazons on the staff, Morton thought, Cardiff prison was obviously no bed of roses. He motioned Price to follow. The guard pasted a 'Reserved' notice on the window; to warn off other passengers, or save them from contamination. Soon the train pulled out of the station, with great gasping heaves. He looked across at Bronwen, sitting opposite him, but she avoided his eye. He gazed out at the grimy streets, lined with dejected brick terraces. It was strange, he thought, that this dismal area could produce a man rich enough to build himself a make-believe castle. That it could nurture a painter talented enough to decorate it fitly; a painter who had then betrayed his ability and prostituted his art.

Morton looked up and caught Bronwen staring at him, with contempt on her face.

'Bastard!' she hissed.

The wardress tugged at the handcuffs joining them. 'Stop that!' she said.

'Could you not undo the handcuffs?' Morton said. 'It seems rather unnecessary.'

The wardress looked at him scornfully. 'What? And have her jump out, when the train slows down? She is my responsibility. You look after your own!'

After that, the journey lapsed into a dull, monotonous ordeal. Every time his glance caught Bronwen's, her lip would curl with scorn.

He told himself that it was less than fair. He had not betrayed her trust. If anything, she had seduced him. And, if Sergeant Bragg was to be believed, her interest was less in him than in his money. Nevertheless, he had been as intimate with her, as one human being could be with another. He had encouraged her to believe that he was no more than a rich man-about-town... Because he wanted something from her. And not even her body, luscious as it was. He had wanted her for her father's talents. In a sense, to prostitute his art so that James Morton could appear caring and filial... And it was no extenuation, that he had not been the first to enjoy Bronwen's favours. An unwelcome thought struck him. What if, even now, she was carrying his child? A possible murderess, bearing the putative heir to one of the most ancient families in the land. 'It cannot be!' they would say. 'Tell the girl to get rid of it! Pay her well; ship her off to America!' That was the usual reaction amongst his class. 'Have your fun, certainly; but never get entangled.' Well, if it proved to be so, she would lose no time in letting him know – even if the child was not his, should she think she could screw more out of him than the father. Morton tried to break out of this self-flagellation; but every time he looked up, he saw the contempt in her face. He closed his eyes and pretended to sleep, ignoring the tug of the handcuffs on his wrist. As dusk fell, they could see the lights of towns flashing by. The train stopped at Reading, and the two linked couples got off to relieve themselves. When they boarded it again, there seemed to be a change in Bronwen's mood. She was tense, now, her hands clenched. She stared out of the window at the street lights, as they sped by. Soon they were slowing, as they entered the metropolis. Price was snoozing, head on his breast. He was relaxed, compared to his daughter. But he had been safely in the cells, at the time of Wicks's murder. He had seemed almost contemptuous of the original fraud charge. And all they could charge him with, in addition, was breach of the terms of his bail. Morton found himself wishing that, whatever they had done, the law would fail to bring them to book. Which made him something of a failure as a policeman.

It was with relief that he felt the train slow, as it approached Paddington station. Another half-hour, Morton told himself, and the prisoners would be safely in the cells at Old Jewry. He would be able to go home, have a hot bath, and try to forget the whole affair.

For Morton, Monday was full of unproductive drudgery. Sergeant Bragg had disappeared early, taking with him the keys to the Cornhill Gallery. He said he would check that the pane of glass had indeed been replaced. But, from the look on his face, Morton guessed that he would spend some time at the murder scene, trying to get his thoughts in order. He, himself had to carry out the formalities of charging Bronwen Price. Murder ... The very idea was shocking. And it was made all the harder for him, by the cold contempt with which she regarded him. She seemed so certain in her denial of guilt.

Following Bragg's instructions Morton charged Evan Price with murder in addition to fraud. Price thereupon demanded access to his lawyer, on behalf of himself and his daughter. So Morton went across to Chancery Lane. The offices of Twentyman & Froude were in the same scruffy state as those of every solicitor he had ever come across. If a trading business was furnished with scratched desks, threadbare carpets, blinds instead of curtains, you would know it was going to the wall; run a mile before you had anything to do with it. But with these top lawyers, it was almost a badge of honour. Presumably they were trying to suggest that their clients' fees were not frittered away on luxurious furnishings; that every penny went on the employment of acute legal minds. But this firm did, at least, engage pretty typewriters. One such looked up at him as he entered.

'Are you Sir John Barker?' she asked with a smile.

'No. My name is Morton. Constable James Morton of the City police.'

Her smile faded. 'Have you an appointment?' she asked.

160

'No. But I have a message for the partner who is representing Evan Price.'

'Is that the artist? From Love Court?'

'That is correct. He is in the cells at Old Jewry. He has now been charged with the murder of Gideon Wicks, in addition to the selling of forged paintings. He is asking to see his solicitor.'

'I see.' She got up and went out of the office.

Morton waited for almost ten minutes, gazing at the fly-speckled hunting prints adorning the wall. Then she returned.

'Mr William Froude is dealing with that case, constable,' she said. 'He is out of the office at the moment. But I expect him back shortly. Would you care to wait?'

'No, thank you. I take it that Mr Froude would also represent his daughter, Bronwen Price?'

'If there were no conflict of interest.'

'Then, perhaps you should tell him that she has also been charged with Wicks's murder.'

Her eyebrows lifted in surprise. 'Yes, of course,' she said. 'I am sure that he will come down within the hour.'

Morton wandered back to Old Jewry dispiritedly. He had got much too close to the people involved in this case. It was the common lot of policemen in villages and small towns. They inevitably knew the local malefactors; had evolved protective shells in dealing with situations such as this. In London the odds against personal involvement were immeasurably long. But, being involved, the best he could do was to master the detail of the case, and try to shut out the emotions generated. He sat down at his desk, took out a fresh piece of paper, and began to list the known facts and the reasonable conjectures from them. It would at least be of help to the prosecution lawyers.

At the end of the afternoon, he received a note from the coroner. Sergeant Bragg and he were required to be at Sir Rufus Stone's chambers, on the stroke of ten o'clock, next morning.

Tuesday dawned bright and clear; the sparrows were chirping incessantly on the gutter over Bragg's window; but for once he did not mind. Half-past six. He would normally have stayed in bed for another hour, read some more of his library book perhaps. But this morning he felt refreshed, optimistic, full of energy. He

161

half dressed, then went down to the basement kitchen and heated some water on the gas stove. Having washed and shaved, he finished his dressing and went out into the back garden. He had planted some beans a month ago, but there had been never a sign of them sprouting. Not that you could blame them, with the bitter winds they had had. He looked up and down the rows. Not a leaf in sight. He gently scraped off the loose soil on top. Yes! The slim green loop of the stem, about to spring out of the earth. Soon the leaves would be there, stirring in the breeze. Summer was just around the corner. Whistling, he turned and went in search of his breakfast.

He still felt buoyant as he went into the courtyard of the police headquarters.

'You are early, Joe,' the desk sergeant greeted him.

'Why not? A marvellous day, isn't it?'

He went into his room. On his desk was a note regarding a meeting at Sir Rufus Stone's chambers. Well and good. Things had moved on a bit; there would be something to chew over. And Morton had been making himself useful. Bragg picked up his memorandum on the Prices, father and daughter. He had half read it when Morton came in.

'Good morning, sir,' he said cheerfully. 'Did you have a profitable day, yesterday?'

'I did, lad! Profitable, if not exactly fruitful. I took Mrs Jenks to Southend! Not that it was like a Saturday, but the oysters tasted the same. I reckon I just saved myself from being thrown out into the street!'

'That is hardly an example to set an aspiring constable,' Morton said with a grin.

'Maybe. But you would go your own way, whatever I said . . . What is this meeting with the coroner about?'

'I have no idea, sir. I did not even see the messenger. The note was left at the front desk.'

'Right. We might as well stroll over; we don't want to get caught here. And there will be hell to pay if we are late.'

The sun felt hot on their backs, as they walked down Fleet Street towards the Temple. Moreover the wind was actually warm. It was going to be one of those years when you went straight from winter to summer, Bragg thought, with only a hint of spring in between. At a quarter to ten they entered Sir Rufus's chambers in Pump Court.

The clerk nodded at them. 'The others have already arrived,' he said.

'What others?' Bragg asked.

'Why, Mr Edwards, of counsel, and Mr Froude from Twenty-man & Froude, the solicitors.'

'Huh! What is all this about?'

The clerk shrugged. 'It is a conference, that is all I know; though there were some toings and froings yesterday.'

'It must be about the Price case,' Morton said. 'Froude is their solicitor . . .'

'Oh, yes,' the clerk said. 'It seems to be causing quite a stir.'

At that moment, Sir Rufus Stone swept in. He ignored the policemen and strode into his room. Bragg and Morton went to sit by Price's lawyers in the waiting area. They looked relaxed – but so they would. They probably knew what it was all about.

After a few minutes they heard the tinkle of a bell, and the clerk went into the coroner's room. A moment later he came out, and aproached the policemen.

'Would you go in now?' he said.

When Bragg and Morton entered, Sir Rufus was stood with his back to them, staring out of the window. There was a semicircle of four chairs in front of the desk; two pairs of two. It all looked rather formal. The coroner swung round.

'I have required your presence here,' he said truculently, 'merely because it is expedient to have someone representing the police interest. You are not here to make any representations, or comment on what passes. In fact, I expressly forbid any kind of comment on your part. Do you understand?'

Bragg nodded.

'The meeting, this morning, is by way of being a preliminary judicial hearing. It will be informal, to a certain extent. But it is possible that the Crown will act upon its conclusions.'

'I have never heard about anything like this before,' Bragg said. 'And I have been to scores of inquests.'

Sir Rufus looked at him coldly. 'I am empowered to conduct the proceedings of my office, in any manner I choose,' he said. 'And you attend here on my terms, not yours.'

Bragg shrugged. 'Very well, sir.'

'Good. You will both sit on that side. The representatives of the Prices, father and daughter, will sit under the window. Remember, you have no status here, except as observers.' Sir Rufus rang the bell again, and the two lawyers were ushered to the other chairs.

The coroner adjusted the notepad in front of him, and picked up his pencil. 'Mr Froude,' he said, 'I gather that you represent Evan Price and Miss Bronwen Price, who have been charged by the police with murder.'

'Yes, sir,' Froude said. He was amiable-looking, with a high colour, as if he lived well. 'There is also the matter of a fraud charge against Evan Price. It does not directly concern Your Honour; but it perhaps indicates the random way in which the police have pursued my clients in this case.'

Bragg expected an explosion from the coroner, but he merely nodded gravely. 'And you have instructed Mr Edwards, of counsel, to appear on their behalf?'

'Yes, sir.'

Sir Rufus turned to the barrister. 'I understand that you have a preliminary submission to make, on behalf of your clients.'

'Yes, Your Honour.' Edwards was in his early forties, well-built and clean-shaven. He gave the impression of power and assurance kept in check. He took a bundle of papers from his brief-case.

'Essentially,' he began, 'my submission is that there is no substance in any of these charges. And that it would be an abuse of the judicial process to press them further.'

The coroner nodded. 'Very well, proceed,' he said.

'In order to assist you, Your Honour, it will be necessary to present the substance of my clients' defence in a general way. Your Honour is unlikely to be lured from the path of rectitude as easily as a jury.'

Sir Rufus smiled warmly. 'I will, nevertheless, have regard to what a jury might find,' he said.

'Of course.' Edwards had a deep, musical voice. He varied its cadences; at one moment persuasive, at another assertive. Bragg could well imagine a jury being swayed by him. But that could not happen here.

'Your Honour,' Edwards went on, 'as I understand it, there are issues connected with the charges against my clients which, while separate, are so interwoven that a jury might have difficulty in deciding what was relevant and what was not. Essentially, that is why I have requested this hearing. In this tapestry of incidents, two other figures appear, who must have an impact on your deliberations. I refer, of course, to Clifford Needham and Gideon Wicks.'

'Both of whom have now succumbed to murderous attacks,' Sir Rufus remarked.

'Indeed, Your Honour. But, before we come to what I might describe as the core of the allegations, I would like to refer to an extraneous matter. My client, Evan Price, was first charged with a fraudulent act, to wit, painting pictures which were later sold by Gideon Wicks. The substance of the police's contention is that Mr Wicks represented them to the public as having been painted by masters of past ages, such as Constable, Gainsborough, Reynolds. From there, the police argue that this was an act intended to deceive the public. They further contend that, since my client provided the paintings, he must have been involved in the so-called frauds. Your honour, it is well established that the onus of verifying the authenticity of an article must rest with the purchaser. It may be that, having regard to the urgency of representations made by a vendor, a purchaser might be deceived. But that does not seem to be the case here. In any event, the remedy would lie within the ambit of the civil, rather than the criminal law.'

Sir Rufus nodded gravely.

'And if the vendor of the painting is free from criminal sanction, then *a fortiori* the creator of the painting must be even less liable. So, I submit that the original charge against my client Evan Price was misconceived and would not stand.'

The coroner smiled.'That would, indeed, appear to be the case, Mr Edwards. It is, however, beyond my competence to pronounce on the fact.'

'As Your Honour pleases.'

Edwards turned over a page of his brief. 'Then, if we consider the graver charges of murder against my clients, I have to point out that Mr Price was in police custody, at the relevant time. Therefore, to succeed against him, the Crown would have to demonstrate that he actively joined in the planning of an assault on Mr Wicks. An assault that proved fatal. I do not see how the Crown could discharge that onus. Further, I have to suggest that my clients' defence would be gravely prejudiced; because the two alleged victims are the very people who could, and would have testified to my clients' innocence.'

'Being?'

'Clifford Needham and Gideon Wicks, Your Honour.'

Sir Rufus made a note of the names on his pad.

'It will not have escaped the notice of the police,' Edwards went on in a reasonable tone, 'that there is, or was, a trio of principals in this drama; Needham, Wicks and Price himself. Needham and Wicks had been at school together; Wicks and Price had been at the Slade together. To that extent, Wicks was in a pivotal position; Needham and Price were acquainted only by reason of their several friendships with Wicks.'

'But Needham and Wicks are dead,' the coroner said.

'Indeed, Your Honour. Now, for the purposes of this hearing alone, I propose to reveal the substance of the defence case regarding Evan and Bronwen Price. Essentially, I shall contend that there is no case for either to answer.'

The coroner gravely recorded the fact.

'As I understand the situation,' Edwards went on persuasively, 'the police have no evidence as to who killed either Needham or Wicks. And, without their being able to lead evidence, my clients stand in no peril under the law. Having regard to the imperatives of justice, and desirous of mitigating the cost to the public purse, they have authorised me to convey to you the evidence they would give, in relation to both those regrettable events.'

'Proceed, Mr Edwards,' the coroner said.

The barrister allowed a dramatic pause to grow, then cleared his throat.

'My client, Mr Evan Price, would give evidence that he was present at the Cornhill Gallery on the night of Sunday the seventh of April. The only other person present, at that time, was Gideon Wicks, proprietor of the gallery. My client had brought a painting, which he had recently executed, of a semi-naked nymph in the manner of Poussin. He stayed for some time, holding chat and drinking spirits. There was then a knock on the street door, which was unlocked. Clifford Needham entered, and came to the room at the rear where my client and Wicks were drinking. By a most unfortunate turn of events, Needham saw the painting of the nymph, and in it recognised the person of his wife. I have to interpose that Mrs Needham had been modelling for my client for many months, and a warm relationship had developed between them. On seeing the representation of his wife, in a most unseemly pose, Needham grew angry. He attacked Wicks, accusing him of betrayal and worse. He seized Wicks by the throat, attempting, no doubt, to strangle him to death. My client tried to separate them, but was brushed aside. Then Wicks broke free and took up the poker from the fireplace. He struck Needham several times on the head, but the man continued his frenzied attack. Eventually, the blows from the poker had their effect, and Needham slumped to the floor. My client and Wicks tried to revive him, but he was dead.'

Bragg snorted in disbelief, and the coroner gave a warning frown.

'That, your honour, will be the evidence before the court,' Edwards went on. 'It is unfortunate that Wicks himself is now dead, because he would undoubtedly have corroborated it.'

'And you are aware of no evidence which might in any way rebut, or qualify, the account you have given of the tragedy?' Sir Rufus said.

'None.'

'There is, of course, the related matter of how the body was disposed of,' Sir Rufus observed.

'Yes, Your Honour. It is a wry commentary on our criminal justice system, that to conceal the body of a child is a crime, but to conceal the body of an adult is not.'

Sir Rufus smiled. 'I take your point,' he said.

'My client tells me that when Wicks realised Needham was indeed dead, he became panic-stricken. He insisted on removing the body from his premises. But, when he looked out into Cornhill, he saw that there were still passers-by in the street. He therefore insisted that my client, Mr Price, should assist him. Together they hoisted the body up to the kitchen window, using a chair to take the weight. Then Wicks went round to Change Alley, and pulled the body through the window. I am instructed that a pane of glass was broken in the process. When my client reached Change Alley, he saw that Wicks was engaged in placing Needham's body in an enclosed van, outside the neighbouring premises.' Edwards paused and leaned back in his chair.

The coroner put his head on one side, frowning in thought. 'The case for the defence is cogent,' he said at length. 'And I cannot see how the prosecution could mount a case to imperil your client, in the unfortunate absence of Mr Wicks. There is, however, one thing that strikes me. The police made no mention of the picture your client referred to.'

'I understand, Your Honour, that my client burned it.'

'I see. So, assuming the prosecution were able to construct a case in relation to the murder of Needham, the accused would be Wicks, not your client.'

'That is, indeed, the position, Your Honour.'

'Very well,' Sir Rufus said briskly. 'Now, what about the murder of Wicks?'

'As to my client, Evan Price,' Edwards said, 'I have already demonstrated that, in the absence of evidence of his conspiring to murder Wicks, the Crown would be unable to sustain a charge of murder against him.'

'But the police are not lawyers,' Sir Rufus said indulgently. 'Perhaps they had a notion that he was an accessory to the crime.'

'Then at the very least, their thinking was muddled,' Edwards said, conceding the point. 'As to my client Bronwen Price's position, I take it that anything disclosed in these proceedings is privileged.'

Sir Rufus smiled blandly. 'To the extent that would be proper,' he said.

'Very well, sir. I will proceed. If the prosecution were able to mount a charge that Miss Price killed Wicks, this would be the substance of her defence. She would say that, late in the evening of Friday the nineteenth of April, she realised that she ought to have taken a painting to the Cornhill Gallery. It was a supposed Kneller, that her father had been restoring for Wicks. She had her own key to the door of the gallery, so she opened it quietly. She intended to place the picture on a convenient piece of furniture and withdraw. However, Wicks must have heard her moving about. Perhaps he thought that she was an intruder, a burglar. In the event, he came down into the gallery, holding a firearm in his hand. He took the picture from her, then compelled her to go with him to a part of the gallery where there was a carpet on the floor. Once there, he told her to remove her clothes and lie down on the carpet.'

'Remove her clothes?' Sir Rufus repeated.

'Yes, sir.'

Morton could feel Bragg stirring restively beside him.

'Now, my client is a very beautiful young woman,' Edwards went on. 'And, I believe, has been generous with her affections; not least to Wicks himself. However, she was reluctant on that occasion. He endeavoured to force her; there was a struggle and the gun went off. Seeing that Wicks had been severely wounded, my client – perhaps unwisely – dashed into the street, locked the door behind her and fled.'

'This is a lot of bloody nonsense!' Bragg burst out. 'Wicks never went with her! He was . . .'

'Silence!' Sir Rufus shouted. 'This may be an informal hearing, but it is still a court of law. I will have you committed for contempt, if I have any repetition of this disorder!'

Bragg sank back in his chair, muttering. There was an uncomfortable pause, then Sir Rufus straightened his papers and leaned back.

'I am grateful,' he said, 'for the frankness with which counsel for the defence has discussed his clients' situation. He has presented their case most frankly and, indeed, persuasively. So far as the prosecution is concerned, there, to my mind, a fatal paucity of evidence against the accused. For the benefit of the representatives from the police, I should say that it is not enough to assert, or even to demonstrate that something might, or might not, have occurred. It is necessary to provide a high degree of proof, before a court will infer guilt. In my judgement, that degree of proof is not present, and will not be forthcoming. I therefore have decided, as coroner, that it would not be proper, or in the public interest, to continue with these prosecutions. Mr Edwards, your clients will be set free forthwith . . . And, thank you for your assistance.'

As the door closed behind the lawyers, Bragg snorted with contempt. 'I have never seen anything so despicable in my whole life,' he said.

Sir Rufus's lip curled. 'So long as the peace of mind of this great nation is preserved,' he said, 'what do the sensibilities of you or me matter? There has been quite enough scandal over Oscar Wilde. We do not want a repetition of that in the City!'

169

12

'So Sergeant Bragg was outraged!' Catherine said. She and Morton were walking in Hyde Park, on the following Sunday afternoon.

'Indeed he was! When the others had gone, he told the coroner that there was not a jot of truth in the whole proceeding. Sir Rufus got on his high horse. He said that he was the servant of a nobler cause – Justice – not some abstruse ethical concept such as truth. Nevertheless, Sergeant Bragg feels betrayed.'

'And the primary object of this fudging is to avoid a scandal?'

'Yes. Tawdry, is it not?'

'We do live in a hypocritical, self-righteous world,' Catherine said. 'Thank heavens that the concept of the greater good has no place in Sergeant Bragg's philosophy of life.'

'Indeed. But it was hardly a triumph,' Morton said.

'But I do not understand why you and Sergeant Bragg were there at all,' Catherine said. 'You took no active part in the proceedings.'

'As I see it,' Morton said, 'our mere presence was all that was required. Our failure to challenge the submissions made could, if the necessity arose, be presented as acquiescence.'

'So the police's apparent complicity would ensure their silence?'

'In effect, yes.'

Catherine frowned. 'But, what I cannot understand is why Miss Price's lawyers admitted that she had, at the very least, committed manslaughter,' she said.

'Apart from the fact that the tune they were singing had been carefully orchestrated in advance, you mean?'

'Yes.'

'Of course, the Crown was never going to be able to prove that. So, as a tactic, it was perfectly safe in closed court. But it is

Sergeant Bragg's belief that Needham was killed by Price. He might have suspected that Price was his wife's lover. When he saw the so-called Poussin, his worst fears would have been confirmed. But, why should Needham attack Wicks? It would be utterly illogical. No, he attacked Price; and Price it was who killed him. Yet we shall never be able to prove it.'

'And what was the real reason for the killing of Wicks?' Catherine asked.

Morton considered for a moment. 'I suppose the Prices were afraid that Wicks would tell us the truth about the murder of Needham.'

'Well,' Catherine said pensively, 'there is clearly no chance at all of my publishing an exposé in the *City Press*. Mr Tranter would be too terrified of being hauled up before this Star Chamber of a coroner's court.'

'I hope you are not too disappointed,' Morton said.

'No. I think that I must be growing out of my crusading phase! Perhaps I am getting old . . . Let us talk about something more interesting. Were you able to go down to the Priory, as you intended?'

'Yes,' Morton said ruefully. 'I stayed there last night. And every second I was wishing I was back in London.'

She squeezed his arm. 'Surely not,' she said. 'Did you take the portrait of Edwin?'

'Yes. And I heartily wished I had never even thought of the idea. My father went all stiff and grumpy, as he does when he is displeased. And my mother practically accused me of wanting Edwin dead! I think she would have burned it, if my father had not restrained her.'

'Oh, dear. I am sure that they will appreciate what you did, in time . . . Shall we go in to tea?'

'No,' Morton said impulsively. 'I have a better idea! A surprise for you.'

Catherine stopped, intrigued. 'What is that?' she asked.

'Something I have at home, something that you might be interested in.'

'It must be rather special, to drag me half across London!'

'It is,' Morton assured her.

She gave a wry smile. 'You are not teasing me?'

'How could I ever dare to do that?'

171

'Very well,' Catherine said happily. 'But if you have been lying, I shall impose a penalty!'

Morton waved down a cab, and they trotted briskly through the sunlit streets towards the City. Catherine sensed a kind of elation in him, a sense of fun that had been missing ever since he had returned from Australia. She could feel her own spirits rising in response.

'I hope that Mr and Mrs Chambers will be in,' Catherine said. 'My character would be ruined, if I were known to have been alone with a man in his rooms!'

'Even if they are not, the presiding deity of the household will defend you,' Morton said with a smile. 'If you can have a household composed only of a single man and two elderly servants!'

'I would be interested to see this presiding deity,' Catherine said, as they approached Bishopsgate. 'Is it a god, or a goddess? I ask myself.'

'Perhaps I will not reveal it to you. It is bound to suffer in comparison.'

'Then it is a goddess! Shame on you, James!'

The cab set them down, and they strolled arm-in-arm up Alderman's Walk. Morton opened the door of his apartment and they went up the stairs.

'Hello!' he called, as they reached the top. There was no answer.

'They are out,' he said. 'So I shall have to put you under my goddess's protection. But you must promise to close your eyes!'

'I promise!' she said, an amused excitement mounting in her.

He took her hand and led her from the landing into his living-room. They stopped in front of the bookcase.

'You may open your eyes now, and meet my constant companion.'

Catherine took a deep breath, then opened her eyes. 'Oh! My portrait!' she cried. 'And I had no idea who had bought it!'

'The sensation of the Academy exhibition two years ago!' Morton teased her. 'Your father entitled it "The Opening Flower", as I recall. If you were to turn it over, you would see *The Times*'s review of the opening day, pasted on the back. What was it they said of you? "No demure innocent on the threshold of life, but a self-assured beauty".'

Catherine felt a blush rising to her cheek. 'Now you are teasing me, James,' she said.

172

'By no means! Who would dare to tease a self-assured beauty?'

'Perhaps I am not so self-assured as you think . . . So, is this the surprise you had for me?'

'No. For that you would have to venture into the spare bedroom.'

She gave him a searching glance, then smiled. 'Very well,' she said.

'Then, close your eyes again.'

He took her hand and guided her out into the corridor, and through the bedroom door.

She opened her eyes. 'Oh!' she exclaimed. 'That is the chest from the Cornhill Gallery! The one I coveted.'

He grinned. 'The very one. When I saw it, I too was consumed with a desire to possess it.'

'So you won,' she said reproachfully.

'Nothing was further from my mind.'

Catherine looked at him uncertainly. 'Are you going to surrender it to me?' she asked.

'Hardly that . . . But perhaps we might own it jointly.'

'Share it? You mean that I could have it for one six months, and you for the next?'

Morton pursed his lips. 'That would be one way, I suppose,' he said. 'But, even though I would gladly share it with you, I would hate not to see it every day.'

'You are talking in riddles, James!'

'Perhaps. But there is an answer to every riddle . . . If you were to consent to be my wife, we would share everything.'

A look of mischievous delight spread over her face. 'Well, it is an exceptional piece of furniture,' she said. 'I am sure it would be worth losing my freedom for!'

'Then, may I kiss you?'

She flung her arms around his neck. 'Oh, yes, James! Yes indeed!'